TRINITY ACADEMY

JULIAN

Cover Designer: Sybil Wilson, PopKitty Design

Cover Model: Andrew Biernat

Photographer Credit: Wander Book Club Photography

Dedication

To you,

Never doubt yourself.

Songlist

Julian's Playlist

Trinity Academy Playlist

Synopsis

A couple of drinks.

A random stranger.

It was only supposed to be one night.

Turns out, the stranger is Julian Reyes.

Formidable businessman.

And my brother-in-law's new business partner.

Chairman of Trinity Academy.

Where I've just enrolled as a student.

Coldhearted jerk.

Who also happens to be ridiculously hot.

Whenever we meet, it doesn't help I'm reminded of how amazing his hands felt on my body.

Yeah, definitely not how I imagined my first year of college.

Prologue

PLEASE NOTE:
*This is a **stand-alone** spin-off from Trinity Academy & The Enemies To Lovers Series.*
Julian & Jamie's story can be read as a stand-alone, but for your reading pleasure, it's best to start with the aforementioned series.

Jamie

Bringing the wine glass to my lips, I take a small sip. I'm not used to alcohol, but when Julian ordered a bottle and offered me a glass, I couldn't bring myself to refuse. People tend to think that at nineteen-years-old you're still a kid, and I'm far from one.

Being ten years younger than my sister, Della, I've always been treated as the kid sister by her friends, even though I practically raised my niece, Danny, by myself until she was four because Della had to work.

I'm really enjoying Julian's company, and the last thing I want to do is scare the man away because I'm under twenty-one. I'm not a one-night-stand kind of girl, but for the man sitting across from me, I'd make an exception.

He's tall, dark, and handsome – and then some. Julian ticks every single one of my boxes when it comes to my perfect man, who I thought only existed in my imagination.

Thick brown hair I want to pull my fingers through. *Tick.*

Deep brown eyes that can hypnotize me. *Tick.*

Strong jaw and full lips that won't grow tired when he goes down on me. *Tick.*

Broad shoulders that will spread my thighs wide open. *Tick.*

Muscled body that will be able to go all night long. *Tick.*

Geez, I've never felt so turned on before. Watching him across the table from me is like having my own personal porn channel.

"You have a southern accent," Julian states. "I take it you're not from around here?"

Shaking my head, my mouth curves up at the memory of my home town. "I'm from Saluda. It's a one-horse-town in North Carolina."

"What's a girl from a small town doing all the way out here?"

Not wanting to mention my studies or too many facts about myself, I twist the truth a little. "I'm a photographer and came out here to get some scenic shots."

Not a lie. Photography is a hobby of mine.

The interest in Julian's eyes grows, causing my body to tingle as more heat spreads through it. It's amazing how he can turn me on with a single look.

Wanting to keep the conversation going instead of just devouring Julian with my eyes, I ask, "Can you play any other instruments besides the piano?"

The corner of Julian's mouth lifts slightly. "I can play the cello, violin, and guitar."

"Wow, you're quite the musician," I compliment him, wondering what it's like to pursue your passion as a career. "I've always wanted to learn, but I never had the time."

"Yeah? Would you like me to teach you some piano chords?"

"Now?" My eyes widen slightly before I glance around the restaurant that seems to have emptied out while I was absorbed in Julian.

He glances around then tilts his head to the right, and with a low rumble, says, "The restaurant has closed, so we won't be disturbed."

The suggestive tone in his voice makes an impatient sweet ache tighten my abdomen. Loving the feeling, I get up and make my way over to the piano. Sitting down on the bench, I glance up at Julian. My mouth dries up at the sight of him rolling up his sleeves. He takes a seat next to me and then pins me with one hell of an intense look as he murmurs, "Place your hands on the keys."

Holy cow, it's like the man's been made of pure ecstasy.

The entire left side of my body feels as if it's been magnetized, and I'm breathlessly aware of every movement Julian makes. I do as he instructs and position my fingers over the keys. When Julian places his hands over mine, my fingers move involuntarily, hungry for more of his touch.

It's needless to say that I can't focus on any of the notes as our fingers begin to move. My attention is solely fixated on his deep breaths, his body pressing against mine, and his forearms as muscles ripple beneath his golden skin.

I become lost in the moment, and my hands still when Julian moves his right arm to behind me, turning his body so his chest presses against my shoulder.

I'm not one for public sex and never thought it would be something I'd consider, but right now, I'm more than willing to let this man take me right here on the piano.

With my breaths rushing over my lips, I slowly turn my head until our eyes meet. Julian's left-hand caresses its way up my arm, and by the time it brushes up my neck, I'm holding my breath with anticipation.

Instead of ravaging me on the piano, he murmurs, "Would you like to take this to my suite?"

Would I? You're still asking?

I nod and can't hide the desire I'm feeling when my voice comes out sounding raspy, "I thought you'd never ask."

Julian is the first to get up. When I rise from the seat and take a step forward, he places his left hand on the small of my back. The silence between us feels alive as the growing desire between us makes it impossible to think.

Thankfully the lobby is quiet, but reaching the elevator, it feels like it takes forever for the doors to open. When they finally open, I step inside, followed by Julian. Turning so I can face him, I lean back against the gleaming steel wall.

Julian presses the floor number, then slowly closes the distance between us. He places his hands on my hips and lightly tugs me toward him. Lowering his head, I feel his breath skim over my flushed face. The touch of his lips on my forehead is so soft, I can barely feel it as he moves his mouth over my temple. The anticipation keeps growing, and when he reaches the corner of my mouth, my body is wound tight from needing more.

The doors ping open, temporarily pulling us out of the trance we were caught in. As we walk to his suite, I marvel how comfortable I feel with the silence between us. The couple of times I've been with a guy, there was a lot of talking.

When he opens the door to his suite, I vaguely think he must be doing well as a musician to afford the penthouse. I don't get to look around because he shuts the door and bringing his hands to my face, his eyes meet mine.

"Are you sure?" he whispers, and it looks like he's holding his breath as he waits for my answer.

It makes me feel desired. I've always felt like I had to fight to be taken seriously, that people only saw me as Della's little sister, but with Julian looking at me as if his world would come to an end if I denied him, it makes me feel like so much more.

More than a sister.

More than an aunt.

More than the kid who always tagged along.

He makes me feel like a woman.

"I'm sure," I murmur, and pushing up on my toes so I can reach his mouth, I don't have to dream about being just Jamie anymore because for once I get to be the assertive adult who has full intention of taking everything she wants from this man.

Chapter 1

Julian

I've been at the office since five this morning, preparing for the first board meeting where our new partners will be present.

Mason, who's starting today at CRC to take over from his father, Mr. Chargill, as Chief Financial Officer and the president, closed the deal with Indie Ink Publishers.

A grin pulls at my mouth as a sense of pride fills my chest. I knew Mason would be an asset to the company, and him bringing in such a huge deal only solidifies the fact.

With Mason by my side, I feel more confident we'll continue to make a success of CRC Holdings as we take over from our fathers.

Walking into the boardroom, I smile at Stephanie, who was my father's personal assistant before I took over as chairman.

"Everything is ready," she says as she pulls out the chair at the head of the huge mahogany table before handing me a folder with everything I'll need for the meeting.

"Thanks," I sit down and opening the folder, I glance over the main points I'll need to present to the board. Moving on to the next page a worried frown forms on my forehead as I stare at the retirement document Mr. Cutler has handed in. Just then, my younger brother, Falcon, walks in along with Mason and Lake.

"Lake," I say to get his attention, "Are you sure about not joining CRC?" With his father retiring, I'm hoping he'll accept the position instead of only being a board member.

Lake first takes his seat next to Falcon, before he answers, "I'm sure."

"Why won't you consider it?" I ask.

Lake glances to Mason, who's seated on my right side, and I already know what's coming. The three of them are inseparable and share the same bond I used to have with Mason's older sister, Jennifer before she passed away.

"Falcon's running with the new company, and I'm here," Mason explains on behalf of Lake. "Once Lake is ready to work, he'll take it into consideration to join Falcon."

"That's not much of an explanation," I state. "Give me something solid for the board."

Mason pins me with a serious look. "Lake doesn't need to justify his decision. The board will just have to accept that only I will be working at CRC."

I have to suppress a grin as another wave of pride washes through my chest. Mason has come a long way after he lost Jennifer in such a tragic way.

"Mr. Cutler is retiring. We'll need a new attorney and vice-president," I mention, pointing to the folder in front of Mason. "The document has been submitted."

Mason, Falcon, and Lake open their folders and glance over the contents.

Mason seems to be deep in thought about something as Stephanie fixes us each a cup of coffee. Before he can voice his thoughts on the contents, the other board members begin to arrive.

Once everyone is seated with a cup of coffee next to their open folders, I open the meeting, "We're honored to have Carter Hayes, the chief executive officer from Indie Ink Publishing here today." I continue to list the titles of the other members, introducing Logan, Jaxson, Marcus, and Rhett as well. Once the formalities are out of the way, we begin to work our way through the list of items up for discussion today.

I glance around the table before I say, "Mr. Cutler will be retiring, but as per company rules, he will remain on for a year in order to hand over the reins to whoever is appointed."

Carter locks eyes with me and asks, "Do you have a list of candidates?"

"Not at this moment," I answer honestly. "I'm hesitant to bring in someone from the outside. CRC Holdings executives have always consisted of the founding families."

"Is the board open to recommendations?" Rhett asks, and I catch his gaze flicking to Logan, who is the current attorney for Indie Ink.

I remain silent for a moment, considering that if we gave the position to Logan, it would at least remain amongst the current board members, which has me answering, "The board is open to recommendations."

The meeting comes to a close just in time for lunch, and I remain seated while some of the board members leave.

"I've confirmed the reservation at The Rose Acre for lunch," Stephanie says before she leaves the room to head back to her office.

"Gentlemen," I say as I rise from my chair. "Should we head out?"

"I'll ride with Julian," Mason says, surprising me because he always drives with Falcon and Lake.

We leave CRC, and I wait until the cars begin to pull away from the entrance before I glance at Mason. "To what do I owe the honor?"

"Honor my ass," Mason grumbles with a smirk. "I wanted to talk about Logan West before Rhett recommends him as the attorney for CRC."

"You picked up on that?" I murmur, once again impressed with how perceptive Mason is.

"Only because I was thinking the same thing. It would be better for CRC to keep the position amongst the board members. We all have something to lose if the company goes to shit."

"True." I pay attention to traffic for a couple of minutes before I ask, "Do you think Logan would be able to manage both companies, though?"

"If he gets an assistant, he could. I'd rather hire a new director than an executive officer."

"That makes two of us," I agree. The corner of my mouth lifts as I admit, "Look at you, Jennifer would've been proud."

"You think?" he murmurs, keeping his eyes trained on the landscape outside the window.

"I know." Keeping my face schooled, I add, "Don't let it go to your head."

"Why? You scared I'll outshine you?" Mason jokes.

I'm unable to keep the smile from forming around my lips. "Like that will ever happen," I joke back, enjoying the bantering between us.

After Jen died, Mason and I drifted apart, and I regret not trying to repair the damage to our bond sooner.

"Right, because you're one hundred percent businessman who thinks having a personal life is a liability?" Mason calls me out.

"I have a personal life," I argue even though I know he's right.

Mason doesn't hesitate to scoff, "You call living at a hotel and working every waking hour having a personal life?"

"I don't spend all my time at the office." Mason gives me a cynical look, which has me confessing, "I've been spending some time at Trinity's music department."

Surprise widens Mason's eyes. "You have? When did you start playing again?"

Music was something I shared with Jennifer, and after her passing, I couldn't bring myself to play an instrument.

"After Falcon and I made peace," I admit. Glancing at Mason, I see the questions on his face, so I explain, "Since Jen died, I closed myself in behind the doors of my office, avoiding anything that wasn't business-related. I almost destroyed my relationship with Falcon in the process, but during the past year, I realized I couldn't go on living my life that way. I let Falcon and my father back in, and I regret not doing it sooner."

I'm surprised by how natural it feels picking up with Mason after the distance that grew between us the past five and a half years.

"Jen would want you to be happy," Mason repeats the words he told me when the families met up for golf a couple of weeks ago.

"I know," I murmur as we pull up to the entrance of the hotel I've been staying in the past couple of months. Stopping my car behind Carter's, I say, "Bringing in Indie Ink as investors was a good deal, Mace. I'm proud of you."

Mason smirks at me as he pushes his door open. "Did you expect anything less of me?"

I let out a chuckle and shaking my head, I mumble, "Arrogant ass."

Once we're all seated and our orders have been taken, Carter doesn't beat around the bush, saying, "I recommend Logan for vice-president of CRC."

Where Mason's mouth pulls into a grin, I keep my face schooled. "I expected the recommendation, but I'm concerned the workload would be too much for one person. We have the trial against Senator Weinstock for embezzlement, and even though Mr. Chargill will run with it, we will need Logan's full commitment."

I glance between Carter and Logan while waiting for their reply.

"Lake, you just graduated in law, right?" Logan asks. "Where will you be doing your articles?"

"I wasn't planning on doing my articles," Lake answers. "Why do you ask?"

"If you had agreed to do your articles at CRC, then with your father still staying on for a year, we would've been fine with not hiring another person," Logan explains.

My eyes dart to Lake, and I find myself holding my breath as I watch him think over what Logan just said.

"You'll still need to hire someone once I'm done with my articles. I won't join CRC on a permanent basis, but I'm more than willing to help ensure the senator pays for trying to embezzle funds from us."

"Carter's sister-in-law will be studying law at Trinity. If we can manage for four years, then she can join as my assistant," Logan explains where his mind's at.

"That's four years, though," Mason states, his eyes locking on Lake.

"I need time to think about it," Lake says, not looking happy with the idea of working at CRC even if it's just for a couple of years. "I can talk with my father and hear whether he's willing to postpone retiring for four years."

"That would solve the problem," I agree, hoping either Mr. Cutler will stay on or that Lake will give in and join us.

"Then it's settled," Mason says, to bring the discussion to an end, "Lake will talk with Mr. Cutler and get back to us with the answer."

"I wasn't aware you have family who enrolled at Trinity Academy," I mention to Carter to keep the conversation going.

"Mason was kind enough to help with the application," Carter states. "I'm thankful that she'll be able to study at your academy."

"Will she be staying with Layla and Kingsley in The Hope Diamond?" I ask Mason. Mentioning the girls' names softens the hard look in Mason's eyes. He's been dating Kingsley for a couple of months now, and Layla and Falcon have been an item for almost a year. Lake recently got married as well, and I'm happy to see them all settling down.

"Layla, Kingsley, and Preston will be sharing the main suite," Mason explains. "I had Jamie placed in Kingsley's old suite, so she's close to the girls."

Jamie.

Hearing the name makes my thoughts return to the hot as hell one-night stand I had last week. It's unfortunate that I woke to Jamie having left without bothering to give me her number. It's not in my nature to sleep with random women, and I was honestly hoping to get to know Jamie better because she was unlike anyone I've met before. We spent the entire evening talking about the most random topics, and she made me laugh, which is a rare feat to accomplish. Her company felt natural, and one thing led to another with us ending up together in my suite. Her sensuality in the bedroom was another surprise. It's a pity she chose not to keep in touch.

Forcing my thoughts back to the meeting, I ask Carter, "You'll be at the welcoming ceremony, right?"

"Definitely. I'll be there with my wife and children so you'll get to meet them as well," Carter says, then glancing at his partners and friends, he adds, "We'll all be there for Jamie. It's a tradition."

Hearing that makes a smile form on my face. "Family is important. I'm glad to hear you have such a close bond with each other."

"That's why we invested. CRC's standards align with ours," Rhett says, lifting his tumbler so we can drink to our newly formed alliance. "To our future."

"To our future," I agree. I feel the worry which has been my constant companion since I started working at CRC ease. It helps to know I'm no longer alone when it comes to running CRC Holdings.

Mason and I went back to the office after lunch, and it's after eleven when I get back to the hotel from work. Walking into the restaurant minutes before they'll close for the evening, I make my way over to where the piano is situated in the corner.

I can't stop myself from scanning over the couple of guests still seated, hoping Jamie would be amongst them. I take the seat behind the piano and stare down at the keys feeling disappointed that she's not here.

I close my eyes and lay my fingers on the keys, remembering what it felt like to have her hands beneath mine. There was something so sensual about playing the piano together while her soft scent drifted around me.

I take a couple of deep breaths, and when my hands begin to move, I feel some of the long day's tension ease from my body. The piano notes fill the room, and once the intro's done, I think about the welcoming ceremony, which will be held tomorrow. For the first time since Trinity Academy opened its doors, we've decided to showcase our music department during the welcoming ceremony.

None of my family knows I've taken part in setting up the program. I haven't told Falcon or my father that I've started playing instruments again, but I hope it will be a pleasant surprise for them.

The first song they will be performing tomorrow makes me think of Jen. It's been six years since she passed away, but time hasn't done anything to wipe the memory of her from my mind or heart. We were engaged to be married before a freak car accident took her from me. I don't think the shock of the sudden loss will ever stop rippling through my world.

Jen was much better than me when it came to playing instruments, and I always associated music with her.

I still do.

Being chairman of a billion-dollar empire is no easy task, and my love for music is the only thing that's kept me from buckling under the severe pressure since I took over from my father. I have no idea how he managed the pressure for more than thirty years, and I can only hope I won't end up destroying his life's work.

Chapter 2

Jamie

"Are we there yet?" Danny, my eight-year-old niece, asks where she's sitting next to me. "Why couldn't I stay with Uncle Ledge or Miss Sebastian?" she mumbles.

Out of all of Carter and Della's friends, Rhett is Danny's favorite uncle. She even has a nickname for him. She also took a liking to Miss Sebastian, another friend of the family. Then again, I've yet to meet someone who doesn't instantly fall in love with Miss Sebastian. She's unique and the most inspiring person I know. Miss Sebastian was born male, but with Rhett and Marcus' help, she underwent a gender reassignment surgery. I love how she doesn't care what people think of her.

Della, my older sister, glances over her shoulder and smiles at her daughter. "Only five more minutes, and I already told you, Uncle Rhett and Miss Sebastian will meet us at the school."

After a couple of minutes, Carter says, "There's Trinity Academy. What do you think, Jamie?"

I glance up ahead, and my eyes widen. "Ahh… it looks like a five-star resort."

Perfect green lawns stretch all the way to where they clash with the unspoiled beauty of the mountain terrain surrounding the campus. It seriously looks like a luxury hotel instead of a college.

Carter steers the car through heavy iron gates, and I take in the library on the right, a stretch of green lawn, and then we turn left into a parking area, and I get a full view of three impressive buildings.

"Apparently, the welcome ceremony is a big thing here at Trinity Academy," Carter mentions as he steers us into an open parking spot.

We leave my baggage in the car for the time being. I'll grab everything after the ceremony. Following Carter and Della, I glance around at the campus and students. A couple of times, I make eye-contact with another student, but when I smile, they just look the other way.

Okayyy… seems people are the same here as in New York.

Danny lets out a shriek of excitement and then bolts forward. A smile spreads over my face when I see our group of friends waiting for us to join them. Rhett catches Danny and swings her up into the air before kissing her cheek.

When all the guys form two rows, a lump begins to grow in my throat. It's become a tradition for them to do this on the first day of school or work.

Della and Carter go to stand at the end of the line, and I turn my gaze to meet Miss Sebastian and her husband, Ryan, who are first.

"Aww... my angel-girl, look at you ruining my makeup," Miss Sebastian groans, waving a hand in front of her tearing eyes.

I lean in and hug her tightly. "Thank you for being here today."

In her usual eccentric way, the words burst from her, "Girl, of course, I'd be here. I have to make sure all these testosterone-fueled guys keep their ding-dongs in their pants, or I'll shove my bedazzled heels up their assess."

Laughter bubbles up my throat. "You know I'm as direct as they come, and I'll tell them all to take a hike. You don't need to worry."

We share another hug before I continue to make my way down the row. When I reach Carter, he gives me a serious look. "You know we're only a call away. I'll take the first flight out of New York."

A grateful smile tugs at my mouth. "Love you."

The serious look morphs into an endearing one as he reaches for me to pull me into a hug.

"Love you too."

Carter doesn't say the words easily, which is how I know he really means them.

As I pull back, I grin and say, "Don't worry. I have Rhett and the other guys here, and Miss Sebastian will kill anyone who messes with me." My words bring a smile to his face.

Turning to Della, the lump in my throat comes back in full force. Besides the four years Della was away to study before she had Danny, we haven't been separated at all. And back then, she would drive to Saluda for weekends.

We both know this time it will be different. There will be no quick drive home so we can see each other.

"Are you sure about this?" she asks me for the hundredth time.

"As much as I hate being away from you, I have to leave at some point," I admit. "I'll be home every holiday and during my summer break." She nods, and when her eyes begin to shimmer with tears, it takes a lot of effort on my part to not cry. "I'll be fine. I'm not alone in California," I remind her.

She nods again, then whispers, "I just hate being so far away from you."

"Me too."

She takes a deep breath and forces a wobbly smile to her face. "You're going to have so much fun and make new friends. Enjoy every second of college."

"I will," I promise.

We hug before I kneel down in front of Danny. I've been there since the day she was born, and during her first four years, I fulfilled Carter's roll in her life.

"Look after Christopher and your mommy and daddy for me."

Danny nods, then she pushes out her bottom lip. "Can't I stay here with you? I want to live close to Uncle Ledge as well."

A burst of laughter escapes me. "You can come and visit a lot."

"It's not the same," she argues.

"Who will look after Christopher if you're here?" I ask. "He needs his big sister."

Danny lets out a sigh, "Okaayy… but as long as I don't have to clean up after him."

Wrapping my arms around her, I press a kiss to her cheek. "I love you, Danielle."

"Love you, too, Aunty Jamie."

I let out a sigh of relief that I didn't burst into tears, then say, "We better get to the hall before the ceremony begins."

Entering the hall, Mason Chargill spots us and excusing himself from a group of people, he makes his way over to us.

After shaking hands with Carter, Mason looks at me and says, "Once the welcoming ceremony is over, I'll introduce you to Julian, Falcon's older brother." When he gestures to the front row of seats, I groan inwardly. I don't like being in the spotlight.

Nearing the aisle, I see Layla and Kinglsey, and I let out a relieved sigh. I met them at a bbq Miss Sebastian hosted a little while ago. Waving at girls, I don't hesitate when Della whispers, "Go sit with them."

Taking a seat next to Layla, I smile, "Hi."

Kingsley leans forward and gives me a wide grin. "Hey, it's good to see you again. Are you excited about being here?"

"I am."

Kingsley gestures to an Asian girl sitting next to her, "This is Lee, Lake's wife." Then she explains to Lee, "Jamie is Carter's sister-in-law."

"Welcome to Trinity, Jamie," Lee greets me warmly.

My smile widens as I reply, "Thank you, it's nice to meet you."

Layla reaches for my hand and gives it a squeeze. "How have you been?"

"Good, just a little nervous about starting at a new school, but I'm glad to see you're here," I admit. "How have you been?"

"Great. We had an amazing summer break, but now it's back to studying." Her smile grows wider, and she continues, "It's so good to have you here. After the ceremony, we'll show you the suite and around campus."

"Thank you."

I feel so much better having spoken with the girls, and knowing someone on campus. Things don't feel so foreign anymore.

"There's my man." Kingsley grins as she pats Layla's leg excitedly, then she sighs dreamily, "Damn, he looks good in a suit."

My eyes go to the stage, and I watch as Falcon, Mason, and Lake walk toward the podium where a row of chairs is situated. Once everyone is seated, the lights in the hall dim and cello and violin strings begin to fill the air. As a new instrument joins the melody, soft light illuminates the orchestra. Quickly, I get transfixed with the music, and goosebumps spread over my arms when a deep voice begins to sing. The piece is so beautiful that there's no way I can pull my eyes away from the corner of the stage where the orchestra is playing. I've always loved music, and watching the students perform makes me wish I had made time to learn an instrument while growing up.

Maybe I can get one of the students to give me private lessons.

Movement on the left of the stage draws my attention, and when I glance at the man walking toward where Falcon, Mason, and Lake are seated, my eyes almost pop out of my head.

No way.

Surprise ripples over my body, chased by a sense of dread.

Julian. My one-night-stand from last week. The one I snuck out on and did an early morning walk of shame for.

Dang, it.

Mason said he would introduce us to Julian, and it makes me wish I had paid more attention to Carter's new business dealings.

What's Julian's role at CRC Holdings? How important is he to Carter?

I'm such a hot mess I hardly take in any of the music as my eyes remain glued to Julian. He's even more handsome dressed in a suit that looks like it's been tailored for his heavenly body. A body my hands have explored.

My eyes drift up to his face and lock on his lips. I remember the taste of them. I remember how they felt between my thighs.

Heat flushes my body, and my breaths speed up as the memory of our night together flash through me. He was amazing between the sheets, and I had to force myself to sneak away. I can still smell his spicy scent as sweat beaded on his skin.

He was my first one-night-stand, and the only reason I didn't stick around was that I don't have time for a relationship with a musician. My studies come first.

But he's not a musician like I thought.

I met him during my short stay at the Rose Acre hotel while I explored my new town, which will be home for the next couple of years. I had just finished dinner when Julian walked in. He instantly captured my attention, and I felt hypnotized as I watched him play the piano.

Thinking back to that night, I never asked him what he did for a living, I just assumed he was a musician, especially when I heard he could play several instruments.

Julian walks over to the podium as the music ends, and clearing his throat, he says, "Welcome to Trinity Academy. I hope you all enjoyed our music department's showcase. As the chairman of CRC Holdings and Trinity Academy, I am proud to say that we only offer the best education for all the young minds who have chosen to join our family."

Shut the front door!

I slide down in my seat and use my left hand to cover my eyes, praying to the high heavens Julian won't see me.

Turns out, my hot as hell musician is Julian Reyes, formidable businessman and my brother-in-law's new business partner.

Oh, let's not forget he's chairman of the school I've just enrolled at.

I'm so screwed, and not in the good way I was last week. If Carter and Della find out... Lord only knows what they would say.

While Julian talks about the history of Trinity Academy, I lean over to Della on my right and whisper, "I need the restroom, and then I'm going to unpack my things. Meet me at the suite when the ceremony is over."

I don't wait for her to argue with me to stay, and keeping my face turned away from the stage, I quickly make my way to the exit.

Crap, how am I going to avoid Julian?

Chapter 3

Julian

Once the welcoming ceremony comes to a close, I walk over to where Falcon, Mason, and Lake are getting up from their seats.

"Before you talk with anyone else, let's go greet Carter and his family," Mason says, gesturing toward the front row.

I follow Mason off the stage. Smiling when I reach Carter, I say, "It's nice to see you again."

"Likewise." Carter turns to a brunette on his left. "This is Della, my wife."

Shaking her hand, I say, "It's a pleasure meeting you."

Mason glances around. "Where's Jamie?"

"She's already gone to her suite to unpack," Della replies.

"We better get going so we can help her," Layla says, giving Falcon a kiss before she begins to walk away.

Mason turns to me. "Do you want to head over to the suite to meet her, or should I arrange a meeting for another time?"

Knowing that she's Carter's sister-in-law and there's a possibility that she'll join CRC once she's finished her studies, I answer, "Let me meet her now. We might not get another chance for a while."

Only Carter, Della, and Mason join me as we walk out of the hall. I'm greeted by parents and students during the short trek to the dorms, as everyone tries to take advantage of my being out in public. Falcon is the extrovert where I don't socialize unless it's for business. I like my privacy and hate when people intrude on my personal space.

When we reach the suite, Layla, Kingsley, and Lee are already there. Walking into the living room, I can hear the girls laughing.

Della heads to the bedroom, and I hear her say, "Jamie, can you come out for a moment?"

"Sure, what's up?"

At first, I only see a girl with the same brown hair as Della, but when she steps out from behind her sister and my eyes lock on her dark blue ones, my lips part on a shocked breath.

For a moment, I feel excited at being face to face with Jamie again, but it soon fades as the reality of the moment sets in.

Fuck.

The twenty-something woman I hooked up with last week is none other than Carter's sister-in-law.

A student at my academy.

Wait... is she even over twenty?

Fuck my life.

"Jamie," Carter says to draw her attention, and taking hold of her elbow, he turns toward me, "this is Julian Reyes, our new business partner."

The color fades from her face before a pink tinge comes rushing back to her cheeks.

"Oh... uhm... It's a pleasure to meet you," Jamie says, her eyes first wide on my face before they narrow.

Is she seriously warning me not to out her? Like I would tell my business partner, I had a wild night of sex with his little sister.

A mixture of anger and worry simmer in my chest. The repercussions of our night together could be disastrous for CRC.

Fuck, how could I let this happen?

You were thinking with your cock, that's how!

I should've done a check on her, instead of letting my desire to have her overrule all common sense.

Thanks to years of putting up a front in the boardroom, I manage to keep my emotions from showing on my face. Coolly, I hold out my hand to her, and when she places her smaller one in mine, I say, "Pleasure is mine. I hope you find everything at the academy to your liking."

"Thank you."

Mason steps forward to excuse us. "Julian needs to meet with some of the other families. We'll set a date for dinner next week before you have to fly back to New York."

"That would be great," Carter replies.

I shoot a dark glance at Jamie before I turn and leave her suite. She has another thing coming if she thinks I'm letting her off the hook. I'll come back later so we can talk in private about what happened because I sure as hell have a lot of unanswered questions.

Jamie

Once my family and friends have left, I take a seat on the couch and stare blankly at the coffee table, trying to process everything that happened today.

The look Julian gave me before he left promised nothing good for me, and it's made my body tense from not knowing what's going to happen.

How did I get myself into such a mess? How do other girls have one-night stands and get away with it?

Ugh, this sucks.

When there's a knock at my door, my mouth dries up as I slowly climb to my feet. My gut tells me it's Julian, and I know I have to face him sooner rather than later.

With the intention of reminding him it was only one night, and we should forget it ever happened, I open the door.

Before my eyes can even focus on him, Julian grumbles, "Jamie Truman. Nineteen-fucking-years-old. Not a photographer like I was told, but a student at my academy."

Crap. This is so not going to end well.

Julian moves forward, and I quickly step to the side so he can come in. Closing the door, I take a deep breath before I turn to face him.

"Let me explain," I try to get a sentence in, but Julian begins to stalk up and down in my living room, shooting dark glares my way.

"Eight years! That's the age difference between us. You're a damn kid!" He pauses for a moment, and a sickening look tightens his features even more. "Oh my god, I slept with a kid." He actually looks like he's going to hurl, which makes anger bubble in my chest.

"I'm not a child, Julian. Get over yourself. I might only be nineteen, but judging by your overdramatic response to all of this, I'm pretty sure I've been an adult much longer than you have."

"Get over myself?" he hisses.

The jerk is even hotter when he's angry. That sucks.

"Do you have any idea what will happen if the press finds out?"

"The press finding out is the least of my worries," I state, rolling my eyes. "I'm more concerned about Carter and my sister hearing about this, so let's just forget it ever happened."

"How could you lie to me?" he asks, a frown forming on his forehead.

"I didn't lie to you," I argue. "I just didn't bother to correct your assumptions and left out personal details of my life I didn't want to share with a potential one-night-stand. Besides, you made me think you were a musician. I wouldn't have slept with you if I had known who you really were."

Julian's features tighten even more with anger, and it makes his eyes look black as night. "You fucking lied, Jamie. You said you were a photographer. If you had mentioned you were a student, I wouldn't have touched you with a ten-foot pole. Do you have any idea how your irresponsible actions will reflect on Carter? I'm his business partner. How the hell am I supposed to work with him now?"

Oh, buddy, you're dreaming if you think I'm just going to allow you to speak to me like that.

Losing my own temper, I stalk closer to him and square my shoulders. I shove a finger at his chest, and hiss, "Don't you dare bring my brother-in-law into this fight. I'm not some teenager you can insult, Mr. Reyes. Whether I'm nineteen or twenty-one, doesn't make a difference. Whether I work or study is not the issue here. We shared a mutual attraction and had sex, but that's all it was. You need to get over yourself. You're not as important as you think, and I certainly will not tell a living soul we slept together. Not because of your image, but because of my

43

own. The last thing I want people thinking is I slept my way to the top. I don't need someone like you in my life. I already have five powerful families standing behind me, and you best remember that before you dare to insult me again."

While I was talking, Julian's breathing speeds up, and then he growls, "Just shows how immature you are if you think you're in any position to threaten me." He takes an intimidating step closer, which makes my muscles tighten in my body.

"I swear I will slap you into next week. Don't tempt me," I say, my voice low and vibrating with rage.

Our eyes lock, and the air around us thickens until it seems explosive.

Julian tilts his head, and a stupid sexy smirk forms around his mouth. Letting out a dark chuckle, he says, "You actually think you're a match for me, little girl?"

God, help me. Today is the day I'll land my butt in jail for assault charges.

Before I can answer, he continues, "I've faced crazier women than you, and each one of them will regret it for the rest of their miserable lives."

Knowing he's Falcon's older brother, which means Clare Reyes is his mother, and her trial is all over the news,

I go in for the kill. "Like your crazy mother? Now I totally get why you act the way you do. The apple must not fall far from the tree."

The moment the words are out, and I see the pained look on Julian's face, regret pours through me.

Dang, I was way too harsh.

Chapter 4

Julian

She did not just say that to me.

Glaring at her face, I try to calm down before I do something stupid. As the seconds tick by, my rage only grows. I can't remember a time in my life I was this angry.

If she weren't Carter's sister-in-law, I would destroy her pathetic little life without feeling an ounce of guilt.

There's only the sound of our angry breaths, and it reminds me of the breathless night we spent together.

Knowing the situation is too volatile to continue, and I can't risk my partnership with Indie Ink Publishers for this girl, the businessman in me wins out over my rage.

Giving her one last glare, I walk past her and let myself out.

With every step I take down the hallway as I head for the elevator, my anger continues to grow until it feels like an inferno is building in my chest.

I slam the button, and when the doors open, I stalk inside and press for the ground floor. I feel a sense of deja vu when the doors begin to close, and I see Jamie coming out of her room. It reminds me of the night Falcon, and I had our argument, which led to us making peace.

I'll never make peace with this woman. I'd much rather bury her alive.

"Julian!"

With my eyes cold on her, I let the door close, and then I exhale a deep breath. Exiting The Hope Diamond, I cross the road and nod my head to a janitor as I pass by him.

"Evening, Mr. Reyes," he greets before pushing a cart with cleaning supplies toward The Pink Star, which is opposite from The Hope Diamond.

A couple of seconds later, Jamie calls from behind me, "Julian."

I shut my eyes for a second but then hear a clattering sound. Glancing over my shoulder, I watch as Jamie climbs to her feet after running into the janitor's cart.

"I'm so sorry," she apologizes to the man, and I take the chance to disappear around the corner before she can set after me again.

I'm done talking with her. No one compares me to Clare Reyes, a fucking murderer as far as I'm concerned, and gets away with it.

When I reach my car, I don't feel any calmer. Climbing behind the steering wheel, I shut the door and take a moment to just breathe.

'Like your crazy mother? Now I totally get why you act the way you do. The apple must not fall far from the tree.'

Leaning back against the seat, Jamie's words replay in my mind, only making me feel much worse.

What if she's right?

For the past five years, I've done nothing but chase after success. I almost ruined my relationship with Falcon. Honestly, we would still be fighting if Falcon hadn't opened up first.

My mother almost killed Layla for the sake of her status. It's the only thing she ever cared about.

So, what makes me any different?

I see movement in the parking area and watch as Jamie glances at the cars, probably looking for me.

"Julian?" she calls, then I hear her mumble, "I could've sworn I saw him head in this direction."

Part of me wants to get out and tell her to go to hell, but I remain seated, watching her take her phone from her pocket.

After dialing a number, she says, "Hey, Layla. I'm sorry to call so late. Do you, by any chance, have Julian's phone number?"

What. The. Fuck.

I roll down my window so I can tell her to go to hell just as she says, "I just need to confirm a dinner date with him before Carter and Della head back to New York."

Upset that she phoned my brother's girlfriend, I open the door and get out of the car.

"Thank you. I'll see you tomorrow," she ends the call with Layla and then begins to dial my number.

When my phone starts to ring, I ignore it, keeping my eyes on Jamie as I walk toward her. She spins around and shock flashes over her face.

When she sees me, she cuts the call, but before she can open her mouth, I say, "I don't want to hear it. Save your apology for someone who cares."

"What I said about your mother was totally out of line," she begins to apologize anyway.

Stopping right in front of her, I growl, "You've already crossed the line, Miss Truman. Unfortunately, we move in

49

the same circle, and I'll have to see you from time to time, so please act courteously and keep your distance from me.

I turn around to head back but pause to say, "All you'll ever be is a mistake I made. Fortunately, I'm a quick learner."

Walking to my car, I don't feel any better about what happened and the things that were said.

Jamie was wrong, but if I'm honest with myself, I'll admit I'm angry because I'm just as responsible for this incident happening as she is.

I shouldn't have approached her after she complimented my piano piece at the restaurant. I shouldn't have invited her up to my suite. I should've done what I always do – ignore women and live only for CRC Holdings.

Things were a lot less complicated then.

Chapter 5

Jamie

It's been two days since the fight with Julian, and I don't feel any better about what I said to him. I hate that he called me a mistake, but I know I can't exactly blame the guy after I insulted him. What I said was petty and cruel of me.

Opening my messages, I begin to type out a text to Julian for the tenth time, but soon I'm deleting it again.

Letting out a sigh, I decide to push through and just get it over with.

Jamie: I apologize for what I said about your mother. It was out of line. I'll be courteous when our paths cross and ask that you do the same.

Before I press send, I change my mind and deleting the message, I tuck my phone in my pocket.

I grab my shopping list then walk to the door. When I get to the elevator and the door pings open, I smile, seeing Kingsley and Layla inside. "Morning."

"Morning, we didn't see you around yesterday. Have you settled in?" Layla asks as I step inside, and the doors close behind me.

"Yeah, I just need to run to the store, then I'll be ready for when classes start," I reply.

"Kingsley's low on her candy stash, so we're heading to the store as well. Would you like to ride with us?"

"Will there be enough space for a mini-fridge in the car?" I ask while I quickly scan over the list I have.

"We'll take my car," Kingsley replies, then teases, "You can hardly fit three people in Layla's."

"Why do you need a fridge?" Layla asks as we step out of the elevator and walk toward the parking area.

"I have an addiction to smoothies," I admit.

Kingsley holds her hand up for a high-five, so I slap my hand against hers.

"Glad to hear I'm not the only one with an addiction."

Layla bumps her shoulder against Kingsley and chuckles. "Addiction is totally downplaying your relationship with the candy aisle." She glances over at me. "There's nothing Kingsley loves more than her candy stash."

"You're one to talk," Kingsley teases back. "Your love for coffee easily rivals my love for sweets."

"Then I'm in good company," I say, loving the banter between the girls.

"You sure are."

Reaching the car, we all climb in. During the drive to the nearest Walmart, I make a point of memorizing the route for my weekly run of smoothie supplies. It's a habit Sue got me hooked on while she was still alive.

Thinking of Sue, a sad smile forms around my lips. She was like a mother to me after Mom passed away from cancer. My thoughts go to the diner Sue owned and later left for Della and me. I haven't been back to Saluda since we moved to New York with Carter, which is actually sad. I miss my home town and should make plans to visit there during my summer break.

"Let's do this," Kingsley says as she parks the car outside Walmart.

Walking into the airconditioned building, I grab a cart. We first go to the candy aisle, and I begin to chuckle when I see they weren't joking about Kingsley's addiction.

"Yes!" she shrieks as she places Twizzlers in her cart. "They were out of stock last week," she explains her excitement.

Once Kingsley is satisfied with everything she got, the girls help me choose a mini-fridge. I get everything on my list, including smoothies for the next week, and then we make our way over to the cashiers to pay.

By the time we get back to the dorms, I have a permanent smile on my face. Even though we only went shopping together, the trip made me feel better and gave me hope that I'll be able to become good friends with the girls.

After Layla helped me carry the mini-fridge up to my suite, we each go our separate ways. I find a nice spot in the corner of my living room to place the mini-fridge and place the berry blast smoothies inside, along with the assorted pack of fruit cups I got for when I only have time for a quick breakfast.

I'm just about to change into my pajamas when my phone beeps. Checking it, I see Della's name, which brings a smile to my face.

Della: We're having dinner with CRC tomorrow night. We need to fly back earlier than expected because Carter has business to take care of. Dinner is at The Rose Acre at 7pm. Hugs xxx

Shoot. I'll have to see Julian sooner than I thought. At least I have a day to prepare myself mentally and emotionally.

Jamie: See you tomorrow xoxoxoxoxo PS. Give Danny a hug from me.

Feeling anxious about the dinner date, I soak in the bath for a long while before I get ready. Knowing Julian will be there, I take extra care with my appearance.

Smiling at the dress before I slip it on, I look at my reflection in the mirror. The lace fabric flares out from my hips, stopping just above my knees. Wearing black heels to complete the outfit, makes me feel a little more confident.

Julian will regret calling me a mistake when he sees me this evening.

At least, that's what I hope will happen.

I pull a brush through my brown curls before I grab the clutch I left lying on my bed.

Giving myself one last glance in the mirror, I whisper, "You can do this, Jamie. Be the better person, and be nice to Julian. Pretend nothing happened."

Or Carter and Della might catch on, and then all hell will break loose.

Taking a deep breath, I leave my suite and head out to the car Carter sent for me. Greeting the driver, I climb in the back and adjust my dress so it won't wrinkle.

Before we reach the hotel, I quickly reapply my lipstick then take a couple of deep breaths. An anxious feeling tightens the muscles in my abdomen, and my fists lay clenched on my lap as we pull up to the entrance.

I wait for the driver to open the door, and stepping out of the car, I straighten my dress and take one last deep breath before I walk into the lobby.

Walking into the restaurant, I can't stop myself from glancing at the piano where a woman is playing to the patrons.

My eyes skim over the people until they land on Della as she waves to catch my attention.

I straighten my shoulders and lift my chin a little higher as I walk toward the table where my family and friends are already seated with families from CRC Holdings.

The instant my eyes land on Julian, I have to force them back to Della and not stare at him looking amazing dressed in a dark grey suit.

He probably knows it and thinks he's god's gift to women.

Yeah? Two weeks ago, your vagina thought he was a gift from God as well.

Ugh… shut up, you hussy!

"You look pretty," Della compliments me as she leans in for a hug and a kiss on the cheek.

"Nothing compared to how beautiful you look," I reply and take a second to place my hand on her growing belly. "How's my nephew doing?"

"He's kicking the hell out of my bladder," she says with a loving smile around her lips.

"Just like Christopher did," I remind her of her previous pregnancy.

Carter stood up while I was greeting Della, and taking hold of my shoulders, he pulls me into a brotherly hug. "Thanks for coming."

"Of course."

When he pulls back, he asks, "Did you get settled in, okay?"

"Yes, I even got myself a mini-fridge for my smoothies."

I wave at the rest of our family and friends then ask Della, "Did you get a sitter for Danny and Christopher?"

"Yes, and let me tell you, Danny was not happy," Della chuckles.

I take the open seat to Della's right, which unfortunately places me directly opposite Julian.

I greet all the other members of CRC first before I bring my eyes back to Julian. "It's nice seeing you again, Mr. Reyes."

"Likewise." At least he's polite, and it makes my shoulders relax a little.

I pay attention to the conversation Miss Sebastian is having with Lake and Rhett, and soon, I'm chuckling.

"Let me tell you," she says to Lake, "My chunk-of-hunk is not as good at golf as he'd like you to believe. Just last week, he almost wacked a ball right at my poor hubby."

"Ryan walked in front of me just as I took the swing," Rhett defends himself.

Slowly my eyes drift to Julian, and I find myself staring at him.

The man might have made me angry, but he's still handsome.

Julian smiles at something Falcon says, then he turns his head toward Carter and catches me looking at him. I quickly drop my eyes to the menu in front of me.

"Carter, you're flying back tomorrow, right?"

"Yes, first thing in the morning. An unexpected meeting popped up," Carter explains. "Logan will stay behind for a month to help finalize all the paperwork for the partnership."

"I appreciate that," Julian replies.

A waiter comes to take our order, and I decide to only have a starter, not having much of an appetite.

When they bring the food out, and a plate is placed in front of Rhett, he says, "Shit, this looks good."

"Ten dollars." The words automatically pop from my mouth.

Widening his eyes, Rhett looks at me. "It used to be five."

"Inflation," I shrug, smiling at him.

Rhett digs the note from his wallet and then hands it to me, which has Mason asking, "What just happened?"

Rhett lets out a chuckle. "Jamie has a swear jar. She doesn't like cursing and has been making money off us for years."

"Oh." Mason lets out a chuckle.

"I should do something like that," Kingsley adds. "I'd be stinking rich in no time."

"Don't you dare." Mason playfully scowls at her.

With the food being served, it grows quiet around the table as we all eat.

Every couple of bites, I find my eyes drifting to Julian, and with a slight shake of my head, I do my best to keep them locked on my plate.

Chapter 6

Julian

The dinner went much better than I anticipated, and I'm glad to see that Jamie kept her word.

Rhett, Marcus, Jaxson, and Miss Sebastian were the first to leave, having to drive back to Los Angeles.

"We should get back to the kids, and there's still some last-minute packing to do," Carter says as he rises to his feet. He helps Della stand then moves around the table toward me.

I quickly push back my chair and take Carter's outstretched hand. "Thank you for joining us for dinner."

"Pleasure was ours," he replies.

"Jamie, are you leaving, too?" Layla asks which has Carter and myself glancing at Jamie.

It once again strikes me how beautiful she looks in a dress.

With all those heavenly curves in all the right places, she certainly doesn't look like a nineteen-year-old.

"Ah… yeah," Jamie answers while she picks up her purse, then she explains, "Carter arranged a driver for me."

"Noooo, stay a little longer. You can drive back with us," Kingsley offers, making a cute face to try and sway Jamie.

"You should stay," Carter adds.

Jamie looks uncomfortable for a moment, then she smiles at Kingsley and Layla. "Thanks for offering me a ride."

"I'll make sure she gets back to the dorm safely," Mason says as he moves closer to shake Carter's hand.

"Thank you, I appreciate it." Carter walks back to Della's side.

I watch them hug Jamie. "Call if you need anything," Della says, a worried look on her face.

"The guys are just an hour away," Carter adds.

"We'll take good care of her," Mason offers some comfort as they seem very worried about leaving Jamie on her own.

Knowing I should confirm Mason's words, I add, "Carter, we're only ten minutes from Trinity Academy. Jamie can call any of us if she needs to."

Hopefully, she'll be just fine on her own.

Glancing at Jamie, she cocks an eyebrow at me, which has me frowning.

Don't you dare call me.

As though she can read my thoughts, she smiles brightly as if she just accepted the challenge, much to my dismay.

"And we're right above her suite." Kingsley grins then continues, "Not that it's a good thing. We'll probably get her into all kinds of trouble."

"You're not helping," Mason scolds her.

Carter lets out a chuckle. "No, it's okay. As long as it's good trouble."

They hug Jamie one last time and then leave.

"Why didn't they stay at this hotel?" I ask Mason.

"They wanted space for the kids to play, so they booked in at a resort instead," he explains. Turning his attention to Jamie as a waiter approaches, he asks, "Would you like anything else to drink?"

"I'll just have a coffee, thanks."

"Ahh... my sister from another mister," Layla teases.

Lake snorts then mutters, "God, help us all. You're probably going to corrupt poor Jamie."

"You bet ya," Kingsley answers, wiggling her eyebrows at him. "Guess you're outnumbered now that there are four of us."

Mason shakes his head and throws an arm around my shoulders. "We're recruiting Julian, so it's safe to say the odds aren't in your favor."

It's been a long time since the three of them included me in anything, and it feels good to be a part of their bantering.

I should make a bigger effort to reconnect with the guys.

"We should do this more often," I mention.

"Dinner?" The corner of Falcon's mouth lifts at the idea. "I think that's a good idea. We can make it a Sunday evening thing."

"Yeah?" Mason asks, glancing at Lake and the girls. "Are you all okay with it?"

"Sure," Lake answers while Lee nods next to him.

"I'm in," Kingsley adds, then glancing at Layla and Jamie, she asks, "We're in, right girls?"

Layla grins, then leans her head against Falcon's shoulder. "Yes, that way we get to spend time together even if we have busy weeks."

Jamie doesn't say anything, which has me wondering whether she'll join the group or keep to herself.

Finishing the last of my drink, I say, "I'm going to head up to my suite. I have to prepare for a meeting tomorrow."

"Damn, me too," Mason grumbles.

"Let's call it a night." Falcon gets up and takes Layla's hand to pull her closer to him.

"So next Sunday, same time, same place?" Lake asks as we all rise from our chairs.

"I'm looking forward to it," I reply, thankful that I'll get to see Falcon on a weekly basis, at least.

"Let's get going, girls," Kingsley says.

They all take a turn to hug Lee, and when each couple starts saying goodbye, I begin to feel awkward. My eyes dart to Jamie and being courteous, I say, "Have a good night, Jamie."

A look of surprise flashes over her face. "You too." I'm just about to walk away when she adds, "I'll definitely call if I need anything."

Under my breath, I growl, "I prefer you lose my number instead." Turning to Falcon and the guys, I say, "Night, everyone."

With a chorus of good nights sounding up behind me, I leave the restaurant with a wide smile on my face.

That was nice. Now I have Sunday nights to look forward to.

Chapter 7

She practically fell into my arms.

So pretty, with sparkling blue eyes.

I want to keep her.

Jamie

I've been going to classes for a week now, and it still feels strange. Everything is different in college. The lectures, the students, the campus life. It's a whole new world to get used to, but I'm enjoying it.

After going for a quick jog, I shower and put on something comfortable before grabbing a smoothie and noticing I only have two bottles left.

"I'll go to the store on Saturday."

Shutting the door to my suite with a smile on my face because I've managed to find a junior who's willing to give me piano classes, I walk to the elevator.

I make my way out of the dorm, so I can meet Lisa for my first lesson. Feeling excited, I quickly open the smoothie and drink half of it before I reach the music studios on campus.

Hearing someone playing an instrument, I walk toward the beautiful, melancholy sound, and when I peek around the partly open door, I'm surprised to see Julian playing the cello.

Ugh, does he have to look hot no matter what he's doing?

Staring at him, I'm about to forget I'm supposed to dislike him and, instead, start drooling. But then he glances up, and shock flashes over his face. It's only for a moment before it's replaced with an annoyed look.

Yep, he's still an arrogant ass.

"I didn't know you'd be here. Pretend you didn't see me," I say, then quickly shut the door behind me. Seeing Lisa walk toward me, I smile. "Hey, thanks for meeting me."

"Sure, let's use this studio," she replies, gesturing to the one next to Julian's.

Following her inside, the excitement I felt before running into Julian, quickly returns.

"Let's take a seat on the bench," Lisa says.

Sitting down beside her, it feels hot and stuffy in the room. I take another sip of my smoothie and set the bottle down on the floor beside the bench.

"We'll start with something easy." Lisa plays a couple of chords to Chopsticks then glances at me. "Your turn. Place your pointer fingers on F and G and play the keys six times."

I do as she says and grin even though I'm beginning to feel dizzy.

"Now play E and G six times."

While pressing down on the keys, I start to feel really unwell and stop so I can focus on swallowing the nauseous feeling down.

Lisa places her hand on my shoulder and asks, "Are you okay?"

"I'm feeling sick all of a sudden," I explain. "It's probably something I ate."

"We can reschedule for tomorrow night?"

"Would you mind?" I ask, feeling a stab of disappointment.

"Not at all."

She gets up, and when I try to do the same, I lose my balance and fall against the piano before dropping to the floor.

"Jamie!" Lisa shrieks, darting toward me so she can help me up.

"I'm…" My vision blurs, and I feel exhausted.

Did I push too hard during my run earlier?

"Is everything okay?" I hear Julian ask.

I don't want him to see me like this and try to push myself up off the floor, but my arms buckle under me, and I drop back down. Confused, I stare up, and for a moment, I manage to focus on Julian's face as he leans over me before my vision blurs again.

What's happening to me?

"Did she drink anything?" I hear him ask.

"Only this smoothie. She seemed fine until we started with the lesson," Lisa explains.

"I'll be fine," I mumble, just wanting to get back to my suite. "I'll go sleep whatever this is off."

"You don't look fine," Lisa expresses her concern.

"I'll take her to her suite," Julian says, and with his help, I manage to climb to my feet.

I lose my sense of direction, and if it weren't for Julian's arm around my waist, I would probably walk into a wall.

The moment we step into the night air, he asks, "Did you seriously drink on campus?"

I want to snap back at him, but my legs begin to feel heavy. I only manage two more steps before my body sags against Julian's.

"Fuck." The word sounds harsh as Julian's arms slip under me, and I'm lifted to his chest.

"I... can... walk," I try to argue even though I'm not sure I'll make it to my suite on my own.

It feels like time is warping around me, and the next thing I know, Julian is laying me down on my bed.

"Just how much did you drink?" he asks, sounding angry as hell.

"Didn't," I manage to mumble before everything goes black.

Waking up, I feel groggy, and there's an incessant pounding against my temple.

I let out a groan before I open my eyes, and confused, I glance around my bedroom.

Ugh... it feels like I have a hangover from hell.

Slowly, I sit up and rub my eyes. When I glance down, and I notice I'm still dressed in jeans and a t-shirt, I frown.

Why didn't I change into my pajamas before climbing into bed?

With the frown not leaving my face, I dig my phone out of my pocket so I can check what time it is. Unlocking my screen, my eyes widen when I see that I have a couple of messages. Opening my messenger, I read the first one.

Lisa: I hope you're feeling better. Should we meet at eight again?

Feeling better?

I think back to when I last saw Lisa. It was after she responded to the ad I put on the notice board. I was feeling fine then.

I open the next message, and the frown deepens on my forehead.

Julian: Do you have a drinking problem, I should be aware of? Or is it drugs? In the future, at least have the decency to get drunk off-campus. Trinity Academy is not the place for you to indulge.

What in the world?

At first, anger burns through me, but then worry quickly begins to gnaw at my insides.

I press reply and quickly type: **What are you talking about?**

72

When Julian doesn't respond immediately, I go to the restroom to relieve myself. After I've changed into fresh clothes, I wash my face and brush my teeth.

Hearing my phone ping, I go to check it.

Julian: You mean to tell me you were so drunk last night you can't remember what you did?

Quickly, I hit reply.

Jamie: Did I see you last night?

Julian: Yes, and you were out of it. Keep it off-campus.

Feeling rattled, I try to remember anything from the night before, but my last memory is of when I went jogging.

Jamie: I didn't drink, Julian. The last I remember was when I went for a jog.

Julian: If that's really the case, you should make an appointment to see a doctor or go visit the campus nurse. You were totally out of it last night.

I stare at his reply, my worry morphing into full-blown anxiety. How can I not remember an entire evening?

I open the message from Lisa.

I hope you're feeling better. Should we meet at eight again?

Meet again? Did I see her last night?

Jamie: Did we meet up last night?

Luckily I don't have to wait long for her reply.

Lisa: Yes, for your first lesson. You didn't feel well, and Mr. Reyes helped you get back to your suite. Are you feeling better now?

Crap, this is not good.

Not good at all.

What the hell happened last night?

I wasn't well last night, and this morning I have a hangover, but I didn't drink.

Was it food poisoning, perhaps?

I search for the symptoms and seeing headache, dizziness, and nausea, I let out a sigh of relief. That explains why it feels like I have a hangover.

Now that I know what was wrong with me, I glare at the messages from Julian.

Jamie: I had food poisoning, jerk. Next time leave me to die, why don't you.

Julian: Food poisoning? In that case, I apologize. Keep yourself hydrated.

I'm not one to curse, but what an asshole.

I slump back on my bed, relieved to know I'm not losing my mind because I can't remember the night before. Still not feeling a hundred percent, I pull my pillow closer and shut my eyes. All I have to do is sleep this off. I'll feel better once I'm rested.

Chapter 8

Julian

Feeling guilty for not taking Jamie to the hospital, and instead, just tucking her in bed when she was sick, I stop by the store to grab a couple of bottles of Gatorade for her.

I might not get along with her, but I did promise Carter I'd look out for her.

When I get to her suite, I knock on the door. I wait almost a minute before I pull my phone out and dial her number.

It rings for a while before her groggy voice comes over the line, "What do you want?"

"Open the door," I say, just managing to not snap at her.

"Get lost, Julian. I'm trying to sleep," she complains.

Clenching my jaw, I growl, "Just open the damn door. You're wasting my time."

"Jerk."

The line cuts out, and it has me scowling at the phone until the door opens.

"What?"

I'd give her a piece of my mind, but she looks like shit, so I keep it in, and instead say, "I brought you Gatorade." Shoving it at her, she quickly wraps an arm around the six-pack. "Drink it. Don't let yourself get dehydrated."

I begin to walk away, when she asks, "Are you actually being nice to me right now? I can't tell whether you're a jerk by nature, or just socially awkward."

God, help me.

Glancing at her from over my shoulder, I reply, "You just have this uncanny way of bringing out the worst in me."

Walking away from her, Jamie calls after me, "Aww... glad to hear I get under your skin. Thanks for the Gatorade. It shows you care."

"I don't," I snap as I press the button for the elevator.

"You keep telling yourself that," she taunts me before I hear her door click shut.

Shaking my head, I step onto the elevator. When I reach the ground floor, the elevator opens, and I nod when I see a janitor replacing one of the lightbulbs in the lobby.

"Morning, Mr. Reyes," he says, smiling at me.

"Morning." I walk out of the building and head straight for my car, needing to get to work.

There's a knock at my office door, and then Mason walks in, followed by Stephanie.

I get up from behind my desk and walk over to the table for the meeting.

Sitting down, Mason says, "I brought the financials for Trinity Academy as well."

"Good." When we're all seated, I glance at Mason. "You go first."

"Okay." He shuffles his files in order. "Trinity is bringing in a good profit. Extra staff has been hired to see to the maintenance of the grounds. They have asked for an additional lecturer for the Arts and Culture department."

"I'm aware of that. If it's within budget, they can go ahead with advertising for the post."

"Next, I have a proposal from a shipping company," Mason continues.

We work through everything on the agenda, and when we're done, Mason stays behind as Stephanie returns to her office.

"How are you doing?" I ask.

Mason nods slowly, "I'm finding my feet."

"Good. I remember how hectic it was when I joined the company. It takes time to get used to all the procedures."

"That's for sure." A worried look flashes across his face. "Kingsley called earlier and mentioned Jamie is sick."

"I'm aware."

Surprise flickers across his face. "How the hell do you manage to know everything?"

"I'm all-knowing," I joke, then continue on a more serious note, "I ran into Jamie last night and checked on her this morning. I'm sure she'll be fine."

She gave me enough attitude to convince me of that.

Mason stares at me, and when I see the question on his face, I quickly add, "I was at Trinity to play the cello. Don't even think of whatever you're thinking now."

"Think what?" he asks, the corner of his mouth lifting in a smirk.

"Mace, she's practically a kid. I have zero interest."

"Yeah?"

He keeps staring at me until I shake my head. "I ran into her. She needed help, so I made sure she got to her suite safely. That's all there was to it."

"I didn't say there was more to it," he says as he lets out a chuckle.

He leans a little forward, a resolute look settling on his face. I'm well aware of how intimidating most people find Mason when he gets serious, but having known him all his life, it doesn't affect me in the slightest.

"You should start dating again, Julian. It's time for you to move on."

"It's not because of Jen that I don't date," I explain, knowing if I don't say something, he won't stop. "I just haven't met anyone who piques my interest."

"Jennifer was practically perfect," Mason boasts, drawing a chuckle from me.

"She was," I agree.

"And Jamie?"

"What about her?" I ask, not happy he's brought her up again.

"It might be my imagination, but I could swear I felt some tension between the two of you during dinner on Sunday."

"Definitely your imagination," I say, hoping no one else picked up on any vibes between Jamie and me.

"Hmm." Mason leans back in his chair, a slight smile resting on his face. "She's beautiful and comes from a good family. No one would blame you if you were interested in her."

"Mace, what's with the third-degree about the girl?" I ask, needing to kill the seed before it grows any further.

"I just want to see you happy."

"Not with some kid. She's eight years younger than me," I state.

"So, you did the calculation already," he jokes. "Stephanie is twelve years younger than your father."

Surprised, I ask, "Have they made their relationship public?"

He lets out a burst of laughter. "No, of course not. But anyone can see they only have eyes for each other." Mason begins to gather all his files, and as he gets up, he says, "Age is only a number. You're both adults. If you like the girl, go for it."

"I don't like her. She annoys me," I say with finality, needing to lay this subject to rest.

As Mason walks to the door, he adds, "Kingsley used to annoy the hell out of me as well, now look at us."

"Go back to work, Mason," I call after him, shaking my head.

Who would've thought I'd have a heart to heart with Mason about women?

Chapter 9

Jamie

After the bout of food poisoning, I'm feeling much better. I get ready for a date with Layla, Kingsley, and Lee, happy that I'll be spending some time with them.

When I'm ready, I head up to the top floor. Knocking on their door, I'm surprised when a guy opens for me.

"Oh, hey. Is Layla or Kingsley here?"

He steps to the side. "Yes, let me call them. Come in." He begins to walk away, then stops and awkwardly turns back to me. "I'm Preston Culpepper."

"Nice to meet you." I reach out a hand to him, knowing that if he's sharing a suite with the girls, he must be important to Trinity Academy in some way. I've been learning about how the hierarchy works around here, seeing as students treat me with caution because I have a suite in The Hope Diamond building. When Preston takes my hand, I add, "I'm Jamie Truman."

Pulling his hand away from mine, he walks toward one of the rooms and knocking on the door, says, "Kingsley, Jamie is here."

"I'll be right out," she calls from inside.

Turning back to me, Preston gestures to the sofa. "Take a seat while you wait."

"Thanks." Before he can head back to his own room, I say, "You share the penthouse with Layla and Kingsley, so I assume you know Falcon, Mason, and Lake."

Preston takes a seat across from me. "Oh yes, I'm their assistant."

"Oh, cool, then you'll know who my family is. That's a relief, not having to explain it again."

Preston lets out a chuckle, relaxing a little. "Yes, I know." He gestures in the air. "The way things work at Trinity is intimidating at first, and it doesn't help that everyone wants to know everything about you. No such thing as privacy here."

I laugh because it's so true. "It's a different way of life. I come from a small town, so I'm not used to the world of the rich and famous."

"You do? Which town? I got into Trinity on a scholarship. Luckily, I also got chosen as Lake's assistant,"

Preston blurts the words out so fast, I have to wait for him to finish before I can answer, "I was born in Saluda and lived there until I was fifteen."

Before I can ask another question, Layla comes out of her room. "Did he at least offer you something to drink while you were waiting," she teases, which makes a blush push up Preston's neck.

He has this whole hot nerd look going on, which makes the blush endearing.

Yep, I can see him unknowingly breaking hearts wherever he goes.

Not wanting Preston to feel uncomfortable around me, I say, "It's okay, I'm not thirsty."

Kingsley comes out of her room. "Are you ready? Lee said she'd meet us at the spa."

"We were waiting for you," Layla teases her.

"Hey, it takes time to straighten my hair."

"Don't I know," Layla says with a chuckle.

"I see you met Preston." Kingsley goes to sit next to him and throws her arm around his shoulders. "He's my hero after saving my life earlier this year."

"He did?" I ask, surprised by what Kingsley just said.

"Yep, I can't swim for shit and fell into the pool. If he hadn't jumped in, I'd be toast."

Shocked by what happened, I ask, "But you're okay after what happened?"

"Yeah, I was lucky."

"Have you heard of Serena Weinstock?" Layla asks as she takes a seat next to me.

"No, should I have?"

"She's the one who pushed Kingsley in the pool, and she also put me in ICU with an allergic reaction. Oh, for future knowledge, I'm allergic to strawberries."

"And apples…" Kingsley adds, then waves a hand, "basically just don't give her anything with fruit in it. It's safer that way."

"I'll remember." I give Layla's hand a quick squeeze, then ask, "Where's Serena now, just, so I know to avoid her?"

"She's been expelled," Layla offers the information.

"And she's serving a two-year community service sentence," Kingsley adds.

"Only two years?" I ask. "That's a light sentence if you ask me."

"She comes from a long line of senators. Money can buy you out of anything in California," Preston says, a disgruntled look on his face.

"She was also influenced by Clare Reyes. I don't think Serena would've had the guts to hurt us if she didn't have Clare backing her," Layla says, surprising the hell out of me once again.

This is information overload, but I'm glad they're telling me.

"I've heard Clare is on trial for attempted murder," I say, then glancing at Layla and Kingsley, I ask, "So it's for what she did to the two of you?"

"Just for what she did to Layla. We only have proof that she was the mastermind behind attempting to take Layla's life."

"Holy cow. I hope they put her away for life."

Knowing the full story behind what happened, I feel even worse for comparing Julian to his mother. It must be hard on him and Falcon, having their mother stand trial, and I just rubbed salt in the wound.

"I'll be happy if she gets ten years with how easy it is to buy yourself out of trouble," Layla says drily, then getting up, she smiles, "That's enough talking about all the drama. Let's get going, or we'll be late for our appointment."

Kingsley jumps up and excitedly claps her hands. "Time for mani's and pedi's." Looking at Preston, she asks, "You want to join us?"

A frazzled look settles on his face. "Ah…uhm…no."

His response makes us laugh. "Poor Preston," I say as we walk to the door. "It must be hard living with two women."

"You have no idea," he mumbles from under his breath, then calls after us, "Enjoy the spa."

After being pampered at the spa, I feel relaxed and ready for a nap.

When we get back to the dorms and climb out of the car, I say, "Thanks, girls, I really enjoyed the afternoon."

Kinglsey stretches her arms and yawns, "I'm going to sleep."

"Isn't Mason picking you up at six?" Layla asks.

"I'll set my alarm for five-fifty."

I let out a chuckle. "I'd never be able to get ready in ten minutes."

"Neither will Kingsley," Layla teases. "She's going to make Mason wait."

"Well, luckily, I'm single, and I don't have to worry about things like that," I say as we walk into our dorm.

"We should find you a man," Kingsley says, a determined look settling on her face.

"No, thank you. I'm happy with my single status."

Stepping into the elevator, I can see my words fell on deaf ears.

"It's a pity Preston just met someone." Layla looks at Kingsley, then asks, "What about Julian?"

"Hell no," the words burst from me.

"Why not?" Kingsley asks. "He's good-looking, wealthy… ah… he's…" her words trail away as she tries to think of more attributes.

"Exactly," I state. "I like my men with an actual beating heart."

"What does that mean?" Layla gives me an inquisitive look. "Did you and Julian have a fallout?"

"No," I lie as the door opens on my floor. "He just seems cold and arrogant."

"So did Falcon," Layla says. "Until I got to know him better."

The girls walk with me, and I let us into my suite.

"All the Reyes' men are like that," Layla continues when we take a seat. "They all put up a front to the world, but once you get past it, you'll see they're actually caring."

Yeah, no way I can see Julian being caring.

He did bring you Gatorade the other day.

And made sure you got safely back to your suit.

Still, that was because he felt obligated to.

"He was engaged to Mason's older sister," Kingsley gives me more information about Julian. "She passed away before their wedding."

What? Holy cow!

Understanding begins to dawn in my heart. Having lost so many of my own loved ones, I know how much it hurts.

"From what Falcon told me, Julian closed off after Jennifer passed," Layla murmurs, a sad look on her face. "Things have gotten better, though."

"So, you're telling me the coldhearted jerk routine is all an act?" I ask, wondering if my first impression of Julian was an actual peek behind the wall he has up around him.

The night of our one-night-stand Julian was a gentleman. We laughed and talked about the most random topics, and later, he was amazing in bed. Remembering the night reminds me of what I felt back then before our fight squashed all the fuzzy feelings like a bug.

"Yep, it's all an act if you ask me," Layla confirms. "Don't let him fool you into believing otherwise."

"Still, he's the chairman of CRC. I think Carter would have a heart attack if I just looked in Julian's direction," I state the facts because even if I liked the man, there's no way we could be together.

"Why wouldn't your brother-in-law approve of Julian?" Kingsley asks. "I'd think it would actually help solidify the partnership."

"Kingsley has a point." Layla pins me with a serious look. "Besides, it's no one's choice to make but your own. If I had listened to people, I wouldn't have Falcon now."

"I know."

If I'm honest with myself, I'm only using Carter as a barrier to hide behind. I just don't want to open myself up for potential hurt. What if I let a man into my life, and we end up separating like Della and Carter did? I might not be as lucky as them to get a second chance at love with the man.

Or what if things work out and I lose him the way I lost my parents, and Julian lost Jennifer?

What if I get cancer like Mom?

There are too many what ifs.

"I'm just not looking for a relationship right now," I say, needing to end this conversation.

"Well, just say the word, and we'll help set you up with someone," Kingsley says as she gets up. "I'm gonna go take that nap now."

"Thanks for today. It was fun, and I hope we get to do it again soon," I say as I let them out.

"Oh," Layla turns before I can shut the door, "remember dinner tomorrow night with the group. You can ride with us."

"Thanks, it's at seven, right?" I ask, to be sure.

"Yeah, see you then."

I wave at the girls before I push the door closed, then walk to my room so I can put on a pair of sweats and a t-shirt.

Pulling the drawer open, I frown when instead of sweats, I see my underwear.

"Huh?"

Opening the other drawers, nothing is where I put it.

"What the hell?"

Glancing around the room, I notice my alarm clock is on the other stand. As I move around the suite, my worry begins to grow when I find one thing after the other that's been moved from where I placed it.

"Someone was in here," I whisper as my anxiety spikes. Grabbing my phone from where I left it to charge, I immediately leave the suite and rush out of the building. Once I'm outside, I run towards the office so I can report it.

Chapter 10

Julian

I frown when my personal phone starts ringing. I come into work on Saturdays because it's quiet and I get a lot more done than during the week.

Seeing it's Falcon, I answer, "Hi, what's wrong?"

"Do I only call you when somethings wrong?"

"Yes." I lean back, a smile forming on my face.

"I'll change that, but first, we just got a call from the security team at Trinity. Someone has broken into Jamie's suite. Mason, Lake, and I are on our way to deal with it. I just thought you should know."

Frowning, I get up from my chair. "Have them check the campus' security footage. I'll meet you there."

"Don't worry, you don't need to come."

"I'm already on my way. See you in ten minutes."

I cut the call and jog to the elevator. Once I get to my car, I wonder whether I should let Carter know. I don't want to cause him unnecessary worry.

I stop my car right in front of The Hope Diamond and getting out, I walk over to the head of security who's talking to other members of his staff.

"What happened?"

"Mr. Reyes," his eyes widen with shock from seeing me here, which is no surprise as I let Falcon and the guys deal with everything regarding Trinity. "Miss Truman reported a break-in, but nothing's been taken, and there's no sign of forced entry."

Stephanie comes walking out of the dorm, and with a nod to the head of security, I turn away from them.

"I've made sure the press doesn't get wind of what happened," she says before I can ask. This is why she's so valuable to the company. You never have to ask her to do anything, she just takes care of problems as they arise.

"And the break-in?"

Stephanie shrugs, which is unusual for her. "It doesn't look like someone broke in, Julian. Jamie says all her stuff has been moved around, but nothing is missing."

What?

"Maybe it's another student playing a prank on her?" Stephanie offers her thoughts.

"Is Falcon up there with her?" I ask.

"Yes, and Mason and Lake are there as well, along with the girls."

"Good, then I'll head back to the office. Thanks for taking care of this," I say as I begin to walk back to my car, upset that I rushed over for nothing.

The rest of my weekend is uneventful until I walk into the restaurant on Sunday for dinner.

Being the last one to arrive, I have no choice but to take the open chair next to Jamie.

"Evening everyone," I greet as I sit down.

The group responds, and out of courtesy, I glance at Jamie. "Is everything okay after the break-in?"

"Yes, thank you. It was just weird."

"Probably a prank." I turn my attention away from her only to meet Mason's eyes. He smirks, which has me shaking my head.

Much to my ire, Kingsley stares dreamily at Jamie and me. "You guys would make such a good-looking couple."

I'm still searching for words, when Jamie responds, "Hell no. I'd rather remain single for the rest of my life, thank you very much."

I should be thankful that she's trying to put an end to the subject, but feeling offended, I say, "You were never an option, to begin with."

"Ouch," Layla jumps in.

"This looks so familiar," Lake adds. "It feels like I'm watching Mason and Kingsley again."

"Right?" Mason asks. "I'm glad I'm not the only one who noticed."

"Noticed what?" Falcon asks, glancing between Jamie and me.

"This went south fast," Jamie mutters under her breath to me.

"All because you couldn't keep quiet," I lay the blame at her feet.

She turns in her seat and scowls at me. "Do you ever take accountability for anything in your life?"

"What's that supposed to mean?" I ask, the irritation in me growing at rapid speed.

"You're so quick to blame me for everything. Ever thought that it takes two to tango?"

"Tango?" Lake asks, yanking my attention back to the group. A smile begins to form around his lips. "Who tangoed with who?"

"No one," I snap, and where it used to work in the past, it has zero effect now because Lake's damn smile just keeps getting bigger.

"Ooooh... did something happen we don't know about?" Kingsley joins in.

I let out a groan, knowing there's no way of stopping this trainwreck from happening.

"Something happened," Falcon says, leaning forward and resting his arms on the table. "Care to share, big brother?"

I let out a hopeless chuckle, shaking my head.

"Fine, I'll take the fall for this one. But the next one is totally on you," Jamie says. I turn to her, and before I can do something stupid like slapping my hand over her mouth like a damn kid, she blurts it all out, "We had a one-night-stand, and it traumatized Julian. He's been a jerk ever since." She gives me a pleased grin. "Oh, don't tell my family. I'd rather leave that bomb for Julian to drop."

Holy shit. There's no stopping this woman.

Is she fucking insane?

The waitress interrupts us to take our drinks order. "Whiskey," I manage to say without growling.

"You should bring a bottle, it looks like he's going to need it," Jamie interjects next to me.

Locking eyes with her, I growl, "Could you stop?"

"Why? It's the truth. I'd drink if I could, but I can't."

"Like that has stopped you before," I bite out.

Once all the orders have been placed, I glance around the table, then snap, "Can we talk about something else?"

"Why?" Kingsley asks. "This is so much more fun."

"I agree," Falcon adds, a wide smile on his face.

Lake begins to chuckle, which means he'll soon be laughing his ass off at my expense.

"I'm confused," Lee says. I suppress letting out a groan because she's the quiet one in the group, and if she starts asking questions, I know the others won't shut up. "Did they spend a night together?"

"Yeah," Lake answers her. I keep forgetting Lee is still getting used to our ways and language, which is why Lake explains, "One-night-stand means they slept together."

"Thanks for explaining that," I mutter sarcastically.

"You told us you weren't interested in Julian," Kingsley puts Jamie on the spot.

Raising an eyebrow, I look at Jamie.

She gives me a too-sweet smile. "I meant it. One mistake was enough for me to learn the lesson."

I clench my jaw as she throws my own words back at me.

"This is the denial stage, right, Lake?" Mason asks.

"Yep, and by the look of it, it's still in the beginning phase. We caught the show in time."

"What would Mason say right now?" I ask, then giving Falcon, Mason, and Lake a glare, I say, "Fuckers, the whole lot of you."

Lake begins to laugh, and soon, Falcon and Mason are wiping tears from their eyes.

Even though my entire personal life has just been pulled apart at the table for all to see, I can't help but smile as well.

It feels like I took another couple of steps forward in repairing my relationship with the guys.

"Why are you smiling. You know they're laughing at you, right?" Jamie whispers, so only I'll hear.

"At us," I correct her. "They're laughing at us because that's how ridiculous the whole situation is."

"Didn't feel ridiculous when you almost took off my head," she mumbles. "Or when you went down on me."

"Fuck, could you not talk about that where people can hear?"

"Why? They already know," she challenges me.

Leaning closer, I say, "Not the sordid details, Jamie. Have a little bit more class."

She lifts her chin. "The only time I lacked class was when I accepted your offer."

Shaking my head at her, I take in the way her eyes shimmer and the constant grin on her face. "You're enjoying this, aren't you?"

She nods, and closing the distance between us even more, she murmurs, "Almost as much as the orgasms you gave me."

I lock eyes with her, and it makes the same intensity and anticipation from the night we met, rush back to life.

"Just an inch more, and they'll be kissing," Lee says, making me pull back from Jamie.

I didn't even realize the guys stopped laughing to watch us whisper.

"Let's change the subject, please," I say, and I smile gratefully at the waitress when she brings our order. Taking a huge sip from the tumbler, I feel the relief as the amber liquid burns down my throat.

"Is that really what Mason and I looked like?" Kingsley asks.

I suppress another groan and instead take another sip of Whiskey.

"You guys were much worse," Layla answers. "We expected blood to flow."

"Blood did flow," Lake reminds them. "Remember when Mason got into a fight, and Kingsley walked out of it with a busted lip?"

"Oh, right." Layla shrugs and gives Mason and Kingsley an apologetic look. "Didn't mean to bring up bad memories."

"It's okay," Mason says, and when he notices the confused look on my face, he explains, "I used to get into fights with West. During the one fight, he fell against Kingsley and busted her lip open."

West Dayton.

"Who's West?" Jamie asks.

"The man who slammed into the back of Jennifer's car, causing her death," I murmur deep in thought as I'm dragged back to the past while the conversation continues around me.

I remember the last time I saw Jennifer. She and Mason had come over for dinner so we could discuss our wedding plans.

I can still remember how silky her blonde hair felt between my fingers. I still remember how her smile used to brighten any room she walked into.

I still remember, and it still hurts.

I take another huge sip of my drink, and when I feel a hand squeeze my arm, I glance down with surprise. My eyes dart from Jamie's hand to her face, and seeing compassion there, makes me feel a little better, a little less alone.

An uncomfortable silence has settled around the table from bringing up West's name.

Giving my forearm another squeeze, Jamie says, "I'm sorry for your loss. It never gets any easier." A sad expression makes her eyes look like deep pools of water. "I lost my parents when I was young."

I didn't expect her to open up about herself, but I find myself interested in hearing about her past.

"My dad died before I was born, and my mother when I was six. Della and I lived with Sue until she passed when I was fourteen. That's one thing a person can never get used to." She smiles sadly, and this time, I'm the one to reach for her hand under the table, just wanting to offer her the same compassion she gave me.

Jamie's eyes dart to mine when I squeeze her hand, and for a moment, it feels like we've buried the hatchet.

At least for today.

Chapter 11

"Hello, beautiful. Have you missed me? I sure have missed you."

Jamie

Things have been hectic with classes and assignments. Having just finished a paper, I make sure to save the document before I close my laptop.

Stretching out, I get up from behind my desk and grabbing a smoothie and fruit cup from the fridge, I go sit on the couch. I switch on the TV and go to Netflix so I can watch an episode of V Wars before I turn in for the night.

Midway through the episode, I begin to feel sick. The dizziness and nausea remind me of the food poisoning I had, and I quickly check the expiration date on the cup of fruit I just ate. When I see it's not the fruit, I check the smoothie and then wonder what I could've eaten during the day that would make me feel so ill.

I only had pasta earlier when I had lunch with Layla and Kingsley. Reaching for my phone, I'm unable to pick it up the first time. The second try I manage, and I struggle to see through my blurring vision as I search for Layla's number.

Pressing dial, I bring the phone to my ear as I lie back down on the couch.

"Hey," Layla answers, sounding cheerful.

"Hi, are…" I swallow hard on the nausea, "are you feeling okay?"

"Yeah, why?"

"I feel sick like I have food poisoning again."

"Oh, no. You want me to bring you something?" she offers.

"Please."

"I'm with Falcon. Give me twenty minutes, and we'll come by."

"Thanks."

I drop the phone back on the coffee table and stare at the TV even though I can't see much with my vision blurring.

Waking up, I feel absolutely horrible.

"Jamie?" I hear Della's distressed voice.

I force my eyes open and wonder why Della's so worried as she stares down at me, her face tearstained from crying.

Feeling drowsy and nauseous, I clear my throat first, then ask, "What's wrong? Why are you here?"

Della shakes her head and cupping a hand over her mouth she lets out a strangled sob.

Carter comes into the room, and it's only then I realize I'm not in my own bed, Glancing around my heartbeat speeds up when I see I'm in the hospital.

"What happened?" I ask, trying to search my mind for any clues.

Not answering my question, Carter comes to stand next to the bed, placing his arm around Della. "How are you feeling?"

"Fine… I think." Confused, I wiggle my toes and work my way up my body. My arm feels stiff and tender, and it has me glancing down. Seeing the bandage, I ask again, "What happened?"

Della swallows past her sobs, then asks, "Why would you try to take your own life? Why didn't you tell me things were too much? I would've been there for you and let you come home."

What?

"I didn't," I say, confusion and fear whirling in my chest.

Looking at Carter and then Della, I know this is serious from the deep worry on their faces. I sit up and stare down at my bandaged arm.

The last thing I remember is working on my assignment.

I shake my head and look up at Carter and Della again. "I wouldn't try to commit suicide. Something else... someone else..."

It feels as if ice is being poured over me as my thoughts begin to race.

What's happening?

Was I attacked, and I can't remember?

Della sits down on the bed and takes hold of my hand. Her trembling fingers skim over the bandage, and she struggles to keep from crying.

"Layla and Falcon found you. They said you called saying you weren't feeling well. When they got to your suite, you didn't answer, so they had someone open the door for them. They found you in time. Why would you do it, Jamie? Why hurt yourself? Tell me what's wrong, and I'll fix it."

I shake my head, not understanding anything, and feeling frustrated.

"Why would I call Layla if I was going to commit suicide? I didn't do it, Della. Something else happened. Did I slip and fall? Maybe I had an accident. I can't remember anything."

"A razor was broken in pieces and found next to you." Carter's voice falters, and he leans over me, wrapping his arms tightly around me. "How can I fix this? How can I help you?"

I hear the agony in his voice, and it makes tears spill over my cheeks.

"You can believe me," I whisper, starting to feel desperate because they're not hearing what I'm saying. "You can believe me when I tell you that I wouldn't try to take my own life."

I cry in Carter's arms as a hopeless feeling weighs down on me. It's too heavy, and unlike anything I've felt before.

I've always had someone, even when I lost my parents and Sue.

Della never doubted me before.

Carter thought the world of me.

And I just know whatever happened changed all of that. It shook Della's faith in me and changed how Carter sees me.

Carter pulls back, and his eyes search over my face. It gives me a glimmer of hope, so I say, "I wouldn't do such a thing, Carter. I've been feeling sick lately. Maybe I was drugged?"

A dark look settles hard on his face, and usually, I'd steer clear of him when that happens, but right now, it fills me with relief.

"I'll ask them to check for drugs," he says, and it fills me with relief.

"Thank you." I throw my arms around him again, hugging him as tight as I can before he leaves the room to go talk with a nurse.

"I shouldn't have left you alone," Della says as she reaches for my hand again.

"You can't watch over me for the rest of your life," I try to offer her some comfort, not wanting her to feel guilty. "You have children, Della. They come first."

"I know," she agrees, but the tears in her eyes tell me my words doesn't ease her guilt at all.

Carter comes back with a nurse, and I've never been so glad to let someone draw my blood.

The results will show it wasn't me.

I just needed a little more time.
Damnit!

Jamie

The doctor just left, and all I can do is stare at the bandage around my arm.

No one believes me.

The doctor looked at me as if I was wasting his time and said a Psychiatrist will come to see me.

"We're just going to check on Danny and Christopher. Miss Sebastian should be here any second," Della says, the worry not easing from her face for a moment.

"I'll be fine. I don't need anyone to babysit me," I whisper, feeling exhausted and desperate for answers.

"Jamie!" Miss Sebastian cries as she pushes the door open. She barrels at me and engulfs me in a tight hug. "Oh, my God. I'm so sorry. I should've checked on you more. I'm sorry."

Overwhelmed from all that's happened, tears escape my eyes, and I bury my face in Miss Sebastian's neck. "It's not your fault," I croak past the lump in my throat.

She pulls back and frames my face. Her eyes look so sad, it's killing me on the inside.

Miss Sebastian, who is the light in our lives and always makes us laugh – even she doesn't believe me.

"I didn't do it," I plead with her. "I wouldn't hurt myself. You have to believe me."

She caresses the side of my head and says, "I believe you."

Her eyes still look bruised, and it makes me shake my head. "You don't. I can see it on your face."

She lifts her chin, and when a tear streaks over her cheek, I reach up to wipe it away. "Let's wait for the results of the toxicology screen."

I pull away from her and cover my face as another wave of hopelessness hits.

I should be praying the results are negative, that there's not some creep out there trying to hurt me. Instead, I find myself hoping with all my might it's positive so that my family and friends will believe me.

Chapter 12

She's mine!

She's mine to keep forever.

Julian

I run into the hospital, still not believing what Falcon told me.

Jamie wouldn't try to commit suicide. She's a fighter.

Hell, I should know, having gone up against her.

When I reach the room she's in, I pause to take a deep breath. Straightening my jacket, I take another breath, then knock on the door.

"Come in," someone calls from the other side.

I push the door open and stepping inside, I see Miss Sebastian sitting next to the bed, her face pale from the shock she's been dealt.

My eyes dart to Jamie, who's sitting with her head bowed, her shoulders hanging. I glance down at the bandage, and it's a screaming reality that what I've been

113

told is true. The realization makes a shockwave ripple through me.

"I'll give you a moment alone," Miss Sebastian says. Walking to the door, she adds, "I'm right outside."

I wait for the door to close behind her before I walk closer to the bed.

What do I say?

Do I hug her?

Fuck.

"How do you feel?" I go with the most basic question.

Jamie doesn't look up and just shakes her head.

I sit down on the chair next to her bed and hesitate for a second before I reach for her hand. I give it a squeeze, and ask, "Is there anything I can do?"

She lets out a bitter sounding chuckle, and then she lifts her head, pinning me with red-rimmed eyes.

"Everyone keeps asking me that question." A cynical smile plays around her mouth.

I hate seeing her like this. We might not have been on the best of terms, but that doesn't mean I don't care.

"They keep asking, and when I say all I need is for them to believe me, they won't." She shakes her head, sluggishly.

"Believe what?" I ask.

She brings her eyes back to mine and stares at me for a while. "I didn't do it. I'm hoping the toxicology test shows I've been drugged and that I'm not unstable like everyone is thinking."

I see a spark of a challenge and swallow hard.

Do I believe her?

My eyes drop to the bandage. "Tell me what happened."

"I don't know what happened, Julian. That's the problem. The last thing I remember, I was working on my paper. The next moment I wake up here, and everyone thinks I tried to commit suicide."

Jamie frowns, and I see the fear blossoming on her face. "It's the same as the night I had food poisoning. I don't remember what happened, just like then."

My eyes lock on hers, and I hold her hand tighter as a new worry bleeds through me. "So, you think someone is drugging you?"

Fuck, if that's what happened...

It takes me a moment to absorb the fact, and it makes a new wave of shock explode inside of me, leaving me feeling confounded.

"It's a possibility." Placing her other hand over mine, she gives me a pleading look. "Please look into it. Can you check the security footage from the dorm?"

Her breaths begin to speed up, and wanting to calm her down, I pull my hand free and wrap my arms around her. "I'll have the security team check everything."

She grabs hold of my back and muffles a sob against my neck. "Thank you. Thank you so much."

I close my eyes because hearing how desperate she is for someone to believe in her is gutting me. I just hope I can find something. Otherwise, we have a big problem if Jamie did really try to kill herself and doesn't remember any of it.

***

"Are you sure?" I ask the head of security after he told me they didn't see anything out of place last night. "Show me the footage."

"Right through here, Sir." He gestures to the monitor room.

I take the offered seat and watch the screen as the footage from the night of the incident plays.

Please. Let there be something.

I spend hours going through footage of the cameras we have in and around the dorm. By the time I finish, and there's nothing more I can do, my heart feels heavy.

Not knowing what to think, I feel like a zombie when I walk away from the security center toward my car. Driving to the hospital, the heaviness only grows until it feels like it might suffocate me.

I've been in situations before where I had to tell someone something they didn't want to hear, but this time it's different. I can't be a chairman and hide behind my title. Jamie deserves more than that.

Walking into the hospital, I clench my fists, and when I get to her room, I close my eyes for a moment before I push the door open and walk inside.

"Julian!" At the sight of me, a hopeful look instantly blooms on her face. "Did you find anything?"

I glance at Miss Sebastian, and when I see the same expression of hope on her face, I feel awful that I'm about to let them down.

Sitting on the side of the bed, I take hold of Jamie's hand before I raise my eyes to hers.

I don't know what she sees on my face, but it makes her shake her head. "No." Her chin begins to quiver, and all I can do is pull her into a hug. "The toxicology report will show there's something because it wasn't me," she says, holding onto the last bit of hope she has.

"Shh..." I hold her tighter and press a kiss to her temple. "It's going to be okay. We'll all help you get through this."

Shoving hard at my chest, she pulls away from me. "Leave."

"Jamie..."

"Leave!" she screams. "I want everyone to leave. Just leave."

I look over to Miss Sebastian, not sure how I should handle this.

"I'm not going anywhere," Miss Sebastian states. "You can't be on your own right now."

"I didn't try to kill myself," Jamie shouts and grabbing hold of her shirt, she bends over as a cry rips through her.

A nurse comes rushing into the room, and the moment Jamie lays eyes on her, she darts to the other side of the bed to try to get off.

Miss Sebastian shoots up and grabs hold of Jamie's shoulders as I move out of the way so the nurse can get to her.

A scream echoes in the room as the nurse injects Jamie with something to calm her, and all I can do is stand by and watch.

I haven't felt this helpless in a long while. Five and a half years to be exact.

The nurse leaves after Jamie quiets down. She stares blankly at the ceiling as I sit down on the bed beside her and take her hand again.

Reaching my other hand to her face, I brush some of her hair away and whisper, "We're going to help you. You're not alone."

Chapter 13

Jamie

Waiting for the results is torturous. The last forty-eight hours have easily been the worst of my life, and that's saying a lot.

When a nurse enters the room and attaches a document to the clipboard at the foot of my bed, she says, "The doctor will explain the results when he makes his rounds."

I wait for her to leave then look at Miss Sebastian and Leigh, who is Jaxson's wife. The whole group arrived from Los Angeles this morning and are taking turns in groups of four to visit with me.

Having Leigh nearby is a great comfort because she's the most logical one of my friends, being a doctor herself.

"Please, will you look, Leigh? I can't wait for the doctor to come."

"Of course." She picks up the clipboard, holding all my medical details, and looks at the report. Miss Sebastian joins her, glancing over Leigh's shoulder.

The silence is becoming unbearable, but then Leigh clears her throat. "It came back negative."

A breath rushes from my lungs as pins and needles spread over my body.

I begin to shake my head, but then Leigh says, "It doesn't mean anything, Jamie. If you were drugged, there's actually a low chance of it being detected in your blood. Most drugs work out of your system in eight hours."

"Really?" I ask, feeling hopeful.

"The tests show nothing?" Della asks, a worried expression making her look older than her twenty-nine years.

Leigh first places the clipboard back and then looks at me. "As a friend, I'd like to believe something more sinister is at play. Jamie has never shown any signs of being unstable, and it's just hard for me to believe she would try to end her life so suddenly." She turns her gaze to my sister, "Della, you would've seen signs, at the very least, some form of depression."

"She's right," Miss Sebastian confirms. "Honestly, Jamie is the sanest person in our group."

Tears well in my eyes because Miss Sebastian and Leigh are at least giving me the benefit of the doubt.

"That..." Della swallows hard as fear tightens her features. "That means someone tried to kill her?" Her breaths begin to speed up quickly, and it has Carter placing an arm around her shoulder.

He glances at me and seeing fear on Carter's face only makes my own apprehension grow. He's the strongest man I know and if he's scared for me...

The door to my room opens, and when Julian, Falcon, and Layla walk in, the conversation pauses for a moment so everyone can greet each other.

"Have you received the toxicology report? Julian asks Carter.

Carter nods. "Nothing showed up."

"It doesn't mean anything," I jump in, feeling highly defensive. "Leigh said it could've worked out of my system already."

"Let me think for a moment," Leigh mutters, and it makes my eyes lock on her. After a moment, she looks at Miss Sebastian. "It's too late for a urine sample, but we could still do a hair analysis."

"It's worth a chance," Miss Sebastian confirms, being a nurse herself. Getting up, she gives me an apologetic look. "This might sting a little."

"You can shave me bald if it will help get to the bottom of this mess," I try to joke even though my heart feels heavy with worry and fear.

Miss Sebastian pulls a couple of strands out, then says, "I'll send the request to the lab at our hospital and let you know as soon as we hear back."

"Thank you."

I glance around the room, and seeing all the concerned faces makes the gravity of the situation hit hard.

Someone actually tried to kill me.

Oh, God.

Dressed in the jeans and t-shirt Layla brought me, I sit and watch everyone argue about what to do with me.

"I'm right here, and I can decide for myself," I snap when things begin to get ridiculous. "I'm staying so I can continue with my studies. I'm not going to let whatever's happening derail my life."

Everyone turns their attention to me, looks of shock and frustration warring on their faces.

Focusing on Carter and Della, I continue, "I understand you're worried, but Della, you're in your final trimester. You can't fly up and down at the drop of a hat, and Danny and Christopher need their mom." I take a breath before I lock eyes with Carter. "I know you want to keep me safe, and I appreciate it, but you have a company to run. You both need to go back to New York. I'm not alone here. Julian and Mason said they would increase the security on campus, and I'll be more careful."

Carter shakes his head, clearly unhappy about my decision. "We can't just leave you here and go on with our lives as if nothing has happened. A crazy fucker tried to kill you, Jamie. It's my responsibility to make sure you're safe."

"And I love you for it, but I'm not going to stop living just because there's some creep out there."

Carter comes to sit on the bed, and I reach for his hand.

"I made you a promise, Jamie."

"You're not breaking it," I plead.

With a torn expression, he looks at Della.

"We can move her in with Layla and Kingsley," Mason offers.

"What about Preston?" I ask. "I don't want to upset how things are at Trinity."

"Preston won't mind," Julian answers.

"I'm sure it's hell for him to live with Kingsley and Layla," Mason adds, the corner of his mouth lifting.

"Yeah, we might be driving him slightly round the bend," Kingsley jokes.

"You really won't mind?" I ask, just to be certain I won't be intruding.

"Of course not," Layla says. "Your safety comes first."

Looking back to Carter, I give him a pleading look. "I'll be fine. Living with Layla and Kingsley, I won't be alone at night." I quickly remind him, "And there will be increased security."

"I also spend some evenings at the music department," Julian says, then looking at me, he continues, "I could take over with giving the piano lessons you wanted?"

"You want to teach me how to play the piano?" I ask skeptically. Even though things have calmed down between us, I didn't think Julian would want to spend time with me.

"Just until we get to the bottom of what's happening," he quickly adds. "Trinity Academy is our responsibility, after all.

"Nah, admit you just want to spend time with me," I tease, not able to resist the chance to mess with Julian.

Everyone begins to chuckle, except for Carter, who's eyes are darting between Julian and me.

"Geez, I'm joking," I mumble at Carter. "Don't go into overprotective big brother mode."

After a moment, Carter finally agrees, "Fine, we'll let you stay on the condition of increased security and that you'll move into the suite with Layla and Kingsley."

Smiling gratefully, I lean over and give him a tight hug. "I'll even drive you crazy and call every night."

A warm smile settles around Carter's mouth. "I'm going to hold you to that."

Knowing I can finally go back to the dorm, I'm filled with a weird sense of relief and dread.

I hope I'm making the right choice, and I don't end up dead in a ditch because I refused to stop studying.

Chapter 14

Julian

I'm relieved Preston is okay with swapping suites with Jamie.

"We appreciate it," I say to him as he carries a box out of the room Jamie will be moving into.

"I don't mind, Sir. I'll do anything to help keep Jamie safe."

"Call me Julian," I tell him for the third time.

"Yes, Sir."

Falcon lets out a chuckle. "Give him time to get used to the idea."

Preston places the box by the front door, then shoving his hands in his pockets, he looks down at his feet. "Honestly, I'd feel uncomfortable calling you by your first name. You are the chairman of CRC Holdings."

"I'm no different from Falcon," I try to reason with him.

Falcon laughs, "We're nothing alike, Julian. You scare people for a living. I'm the loving and caring brother."

"Says who?" Layla jumps in. "You're intimidating as well. It's a family trademark y'all have."

Falcon leans closer to her. "Am I not loving enough?"

"Ah… that's a conversation for another time," Layla quickly puts an end to the topic.

I find myself smiling, and when Jamie walks into the suite with a box, I rush over to her. "Why are you carrying this? Let the staff take care of moving the boxes."

"Aww… it almost sounds like you care about me," she taunts me.

"I just don't need you getting injured again on Trinity grounds," I mutter as I place the box down by the bedroom door, but instantly regret my words. "I mean, *we* just want to keep you safe."

"Hmm… right." Jamie smiles at me, but the worry she's been carrying around with her dims it.

Miss Sebastian comes walking into the room with a little, colorful unicorn sculpture. "Where can I put this?"

"Trust you to make sure I don't forget to bring my Christmas gift you gave me," Jamie teases her.

"Of course, you need some color in your life, now more than ever," Miss Sebastian defends her actions.

Rhett follows after Miss Sebastian with another box, which has me saying, "Let's sit down while the staff takes care of moving everything between the two suites. Mason and Lake will be back any moment with the take-out we ordered."

Only Rhett and Miss Sebastian stayed behind. The rest of Jamie's family and friends needed to get back to work.

I had to reassure Carter I'd protect Jamie before he and Della would leave to catch their flight back to New York. They mentioned they would fly out again this coming weekend to spend some more time with Jamie.

Miss Sebastian begins to look around the suite, saying, "This place could do with a little color. I need to add my dazzling touch, so all this blandness won't mess with Jamie's juju."

Jamie takes hold of Miss Sebastian's arm as if to keep her from getting started on giving the luxurious suite a makeover. "That's not something you need to think about right now. Come sit and rest a little."

"Aww... my angel-child. No need to worry about me. My bedazzled ass has the stamina of a stallion."

I hear a burst of laughter from Lake before he walks into the suite, and Mason has to move fast to grab the pizza boxes from him, before our dinner lands on the floor. I can only assume he's cracking up because of what Miss Sebastian said.

––––––––––––––––––––––––––––

The suite is crammed with everyone sitting where there's an open space. Taking a bite of pizza, my eyes land on Jamie.

She reaches for another slice and catching me watching her, she sticks out her tongue at me, then says, "You better eat, Mr. Reyes, or I'll finish it all."

"Don't let me stop you from stuffing your face," I throw back at her, unable to stop the corner of my mouth from lifting.

I'm glad she has a healthy appetite with all the shit that's happening.

She takes a big bite, and her tongue darts out to lick her lips. "Mhhh… so yummy."

Mason leans closer to me and whispers, "Enjoying the food porn?"

Scowling at him, I shake my head. "Don't even go there today."

"Where do you want to go?" Kingsley asks, catching the tail end of our hopefully short conversation.

"Nowhere," I answer on behalf of Mason, not giving him time to say something I might regret.

Lake begins to chuckle, which has me shooting a glare his way. "Have another slice, Lake."

"Don't mind if I do." He loads another three slices onto his plate and croons, "Come to Daddy."

"Where the hell does he put it all?" I mumble to myself.

I'm relieved the atmosphere around dinner is light, and when everyone has had enough, Lee gets up to start cleaning. Layla and Kingsley join her, which has Jamie getting up as well. She walks to my side of the table and leaning close to me, she picks up my plate.

"Thank you."

I glance up at her as she replies, "You're welcome. When I'm done helping the girls, can we talk in private?"

"Sure."

As she continues gathering plates, I rest my elbow on the table, and wondering what she wants to talk about, I rub a thumb over my bottom lip.

Perhaps she wants to discuss the piano lessons I mentioned?

"It's only a matter of time now," Lake suddenly says, pulling me out of my thoughts.

"For what?" Mason asks, which has Lake gesturing in my direction.

"Yeah, you think?" Falcon asks.

"What the hell are you talking about?" I ask, hating when they silently communicate with their eyes, which can only mean trouble for me.

"About you taking the plunge," Lake clarifies, giving me a knowing smile.

"Y'all need to stop already," I grumble a warning.

"Why? Isn't my angel-girl good enough for you?" Miss Sebastian jumps into the conversation.

I let out a groan of self-pity, knowing there's no stopping her once she gets started.

"Leave him be, Miss Sebastian," Jamie scolds her playfully.

Rhett leans forward, pinning me with one hell of an intimidating look. "Is there something going on, I don't know about?"

"Not at all," I assure him.

"Not at all, my bedazzled ass." Miss Sebastian points a finger at me then at Jamie. "I see the way y'all keep stealing glances at each other."

I take a deep breath and tiredly rub a hand over my face.

There's just no winning with these people.

"Like Julian said, there's nothing going on," Jamie tries to argue. "Besides, even if we're interested in each other, it really has nothing to do with y'all."

"As long as it doesn't affect our business dealings," Rhett warns.

Needing to assure Rhett, I say, "It won't. There's really nothing to worry about."

"So, you're admitting there's something, though?" Miss Sebastian continues to flog a dead horse.

"God, help me," I groan. "No, I'm just reassuring Rhett so he won't worry."

"Hmm..." Miss Sebastian keeps glancing between Jamie and me.

Just as the conversation turns to Preston and his new girlfriend, giving me some reprieve, Jamie walks over to me and whispers, "Can we talk now?"

"You really think now is a good time?" I ask, not wanting the spotlight back on us.

"What are you two love-birds whispering about?" Miss Sebastian asks.

"Too late," I grumble, closing my eyes in defeat.

"Fine, I'll just talk here," Jamie says. "Were you serious about teaching me the piano?"

"You couldn't wait to ask that?" I rise from the chair, so I don't have to stare up at Jamie.

"Julian, were you serious?" she asks again.

"Yes. Your previous tutor probably got a new student by now, and I thought it would help take your mind off everything that's happened."

"Great, when do we start?" There's a flash of excitement in her eyes, which is a nice change from the worried expression she's had since waking in the hospital.

"We can begin as soon as you're settled into your new room. Though the lessons will have to be after eight in the evenings."

"I'll be settled in no time. Can we start tonight?" she asks, a pleading look crossing her features.

Not having the heart to say no, I agree, "Fine, but you better not give me attitude during the lessons."

"Would I ever?" She widens her eyes for added effect.

I let out a chuckle then decide to make a quick escape before Miss Sebastian has something to say about me offering to teach Jamie to play the piano.

"If you'll all excuse me, I have some calls to make."

Mason coughs and mutters under his breath, "Bullshit."

"That will be ten dollars," Jamie pipes up.

A look of surprise flashes across Mason's face. "Why?"

"You have to pay up for cursing," Rhett explains to him.

Mason lets out a chuckle. "I do?"

"Don't worry, it's Jamie's way of showing she cares," Miss Sebastian says.

"Ten dollars it is then." Mason pulls the note from his wallet and hands it to Jamie.

"Ooh... you curse like a drunken sailor. With all the money I'll make off you, we can pay for our Sunday dinners out of the swear jar."

"That's an excellent idea," Lake laughs. "I should've thought of that. I'd never have to pay for food again."

Shaking my head at their bantering, I wave and leave the suite with a smile on my face.

That's something I've started to notice recently. I've been smiling more.

Chapter 15

Jamie

Julian: Wait at the suite. I'll meet you there at eight.

I frown at the message, wondering why he would want me to wait here.

Is it possible he does care and doesn't want me walking the short distance to the music building alone in the dark?

"Aww… sweet. He has a heart after all," I murmur as I place my phone down on the nightstand.

Thirty minutes later, I've put away most of my clothes, and as I'm placing my bras in the drawers, Kingsley calls out, "Jamie, Julian's here."

"I'll be right out," I shout back, rushing to the bed. I scoop up my panties, and as I turn to the dresser, Julian comes to stand in the doorway. I shove the bundle of lingerie into the drawer then close it. "All done. Let's go."

Walking toward him, I'm surprised to see he's not wearing a suit, but instead, opted for wearing a pair of jeans and a sweater. The sleeves are pushed up to his elbows, giving me a view of his forearms in all their annoyingly sexy glory.

When we head for the front door, Kingsley's voice drips with innuendo as she says, "Enjoy your piano lesson."

I smile at her and wiggle my eyebrows before I pull the front door closed behind us.

"Did you manage to return all your calls?" I ask to make conversation as we wait for the elevator to open.

The last time I stood in front of an elevator with him, my panties were practically melting from all the heat I was feeling.

Nope, don't think about that night.

"Yes, I did. Thank you for asking," Julian answers formally.

"Seriously?" I ask, stepping inside the elevator. "Are you going to be all formal now?"

"I'm not formal," he argues. "I even dressed casually."

Letting my eyes sweep over his well-toned body, I tease, "I can see that. The look suits you."

That's no lie. The man looks good in a suit, but seeing him like this is nothing short of yummy.

I notice his eyes moving over me, but then they stop on the bandage. "How does your arm feel?"

137

"Better. Thank you for asking." I repeat his words from earlier, then chuckle when a light frown forms on his face from my reserved tone.

The doors to the elevator open, and as we step out, a janitor comes toward us, so I step closer to Julian to get out of his way.

"Evening, Mr. Reyes, Miss Truman," the janitor says, a friendly smile on his face.

"Hi," I greet him, where Julian just nods his head at the man.

When we walk out of the building, I ask, "How does he know my name?"

"He probably had to fix something in your suite," Julian guesses.

I shrug it off and glance around me as we walk down the path leading to the music building.

A couple of security guards pass by us, each one greeting us.

"It's actually comforting seeing the extra security around campus. Thank you for arranging it."

We reach the building, and Julian opens the door. Waiting for me to walk in first, he murmurs, "You're welcome."

"Which studio do you want to use?" I ask, stopping in front of the first door.

"I prefer number four."

Julian walks behind me, and when we're in the studio, I head over to the piano and sitting down, I look up at him.

Geez, talk about having déjà vu.

My eyes drop to his arms before I turn my head away and look down at the keys.

As Julian takes a seat next to me, and his arm presses against mine, I feel the same fluttering of attraction I had when I first met him.

"Place your hands on the keys." His voice is nothing more than a low rumble, and it makes my eyes snap up to his face, wondering if he's feeling the same thing as me.

We stare at each other, and it only makes the moment grow with more intensity, but then a guarded look settles on his face.

"Let's not go there, Jamie."

"Go where?" I ask, wanting to hear him say it. We might not have a chance at having a relationship, but I still want to hear him admit the attraction wasn't one-sided.

He lets out a deep breath before saying, "You know where."

I let out a burst of cynical laughter. "You can't even admit it. I think it's quite sad because our night together actually meant something to me."

Hey, at least no one can fault me for not being honest.

Julian clears his throat, then murmurs, "I'm sorry I said being with you was a mistake."

"Yeah, you don't look like someone who makes mistakes," I tease to lighten the air around us.

I place my pointer fingers on the F and G keys and press them four times before I stop, an eerie feeling rippling through me.

"This feels familiar," I whisper, trying to remember where I learned it.

"Lisa taught you the first keys to Chopsticks the night you..." Julian's words trail away and glancing up at him, I see a deep frown on his forehead. "You were out of it as if you were..." his eyes meet mine, and seeing the worry, I finish his sentence, "drugged."

I drop my hands back to my lap as the fear comes trickling back into my heart.

"What..." I swallow hard on the lump forming in my throat. "What do I do if there's really a creep out there who wants to hurt me?"

"We'll catch him, Jamie," Julian says with so much certainty I almost believe him.

I take a deep breath and let my eyes glance around the room, taking in the cello, a violin, a set of drums, and every other instrument in here while I try to get my emotions back under control.

"I hope so." Forcing a smile around my lips, I ask, "Are you going to teach me Chopsticks?"

"Yes, it's the easiest piece to learn with."

I position my hands on the right keys and follow Julian's instructions, but no matter how hard I try, I can't focus and keep making mistakes.

"It's okay. You'll get the hang of it," Julian says patiently.

"I'd rather you bite my head off. Being overly patient with me isn't helping," I say as I try the notes again. "It just reminds me that I might be in danger, and you're so worried you're forgetting to argue with me."

To my surprise, Julian lets out a chuckle, then he growls, "Focus, Jamie. Don't waste my time."

I begin to laugh and give him a thankful smile, but it fades away when I see the concern coloring his irises black.

"I'm scared," I whisper, the emotions all rushing back to suffocate me. "I'm so scared, Julian."

141

Turning his body toward me, he pulls me into a hug, promising, "I won't let anything happen to you."

Wrapping my arms around his waist, I bury my face against his chest and breathe in his spicy scent.

After a moment, I mumble, "I know I've been a pain in the butt, but thank you for supporting me through this nightmare."

"You're welcome." He moves his hand to the back of my head and gently caresses my hair.

When minutes have passed, I pull back, giving Julian another grateful smile, then I say with a joking tone, "So much for the piano lesson."

He shakes his head. "Tsk… at this rate, it's going to take forever to teach you."

"Well, I hope you have lots of time because I'm not giving up."

Our bantering lightens the air and feeling better after the comfort Julian gave me, I actually manage to concentrate and learn a couple of notes.

After the lesson, Julian walks me back to the suite. When I open the door, he follows me inside, and I watch as he goes to check my room before walking back to where I am.

Smiling, I say, "Thank you for tonight. I appreciate it."

"You're welcome."

He takes a step toward the hallway, and not wanting to miss the chance, I quickly hold a hand out to him. "Friends?"

The corner of his mouth lifts slightly as he takes my hand, his fingers closing warmly around mine. "Friends."

"Enjoy the rest of your night," I say as I pull my hand free.

"You too."

After he leaves, I close the door and make sure to lock it before I walk to my room, thinking at least something good has come from this horrible ordeal.

Chapter 16

Julian

Signing the documents Stephanie placed on my desk earlier, my head snaps up when the door to my office bursts open without a knock.

Mason rushes in, a dark scowl on his face, and it has me putting down the pen as I frown at him. "What's wrong?"

"We officially have one hell of a big problem." He takes a moment to catch his breath. "Preston just called me. He found cameras hidden in Jamie's old suite. He tried to trace the feed, but it only shows that it's coming from within the grounds of Trinity."

"What?" Shock numbs me for a moment, but then the gravity of the situation sinks in, and I rise from my seat so fast it sends the chair rolling backward until it slams against the floor to ceiling windows behind my desk. "Someone was watching Jamie?"

"Yes," he grinds the word out. "We need to report this to the police, and we have to call Carter."

A wave of anger hits, knowing someone has been invading Jamie's privacy. Walking to where my jacket is hanging, I grab it and shrug it on. "I'm going to Trinity."

"Shouldn't you call Carter first," Mason argues.

"No. You can call him. Right now, I'm going to Jamie. She's going to be scared out of her mind when she hears this. As far as I'm concerned, her well-being comes before Carter and the police," I snap, then rush out of my office.

As soon as I walk out of the elevator on the ground floor, I pull my phone from my pocket and bring up Jamie's number.

"Julian?" she answers her voice sounding shaky.

"You've heard?" I ask.

"Yes."

"I'm on my way over. Stay in your suite."

"Okay."

I hear her exhale a trembling breath, and I add, "I'll be there in five minutes."

"Okay."

Climbing into my car, I attach my phone to the Bluetooth. "Do you want me to stay on the line while I drive over?"

"Please." The word sounds like it's been drenched in dread.

I start the engine and steer the car away from CRC, and not knowing what else to talk about right now, I ask, "Have you been able to catch up on the work you missed?"

Jamie sucks in another trembling breath. "I was busy working on a paper when I heard…"

When her words trail away, I ask, "What was the paper about?"

"About why the liquidating fiduciary exception should not exist."

"You like arguing, so you'll do great with the paper."

She lets out a burst of laughter, but then it hitches in her throat.

Driving up to the gate of Trinity, I say, "I'm here, just parking the car."

"Uh-huh."

Her voice sounds so small, I decide to stop right in front of the dorm. Unplugging my phone, I bring it to my ear as I open my door and climb out. I rush inside, saying, "I'm going to hang up now."

"Okay."

Stepping into the elevator, I slam at the button as anger ripples through me again. I'm going to find whoever is doing this to Jamie and destroy them.

As I walk out of the elevator, I pause to phone Preston.

"Preston Culpepper speaking."

"It's Julian. Come up to Jamie's suite. I want to know everything about the cameras you found."

"Yes, Sir."

Cutting the call, I rush to the door, and I only have to knock once before it opens, and I'm met with Layla's pale face. "Hey."

"Hi."

Walking into the suite, I see Jamie standing out on the balcony. When I reach her, she glances up at me before dropping her eyes to the floor.

As I bring my hand to her chin so I can lift her face, her breaths begin to come faster. She pulls free, shaking her head, and it makes me close the distance between us so I can wrap my arms around her.

"I'm going to cry," she mumbles against my chest, trying to pull away from me.

"No one will blame you," I say, tightening my hold on her.

"I don't want to cry in front of the others," she complains.

I let her go, but only so I can take hold of her hand. I pull her to her room and close the door behind us for privacy.

Drawing Jamie back against my chest, I whisper, "Now, no one will see. Cry."

"Julian." Her voice catches, and instead of pushing me away again, she wraps her arms around me, grabbing hold of my jacket. Her body jerks, and she smothers a sob against my shirt.

I move a hand to her hair, caressing the silky strands, and press a kiss to the top of her head. Not knowing what to say, I can only hold her until her tears fade, and she pulls back again.

She first walks to the bedside and grabbing a tissue, she blows her nose. "Someone has been watching me." Her voice sounds haunted, and it stabs at my heart. "There was even a camera in the bathroom."

"We're going to report it to the police. Mason has called them already," I say, hoping it will offer some comfort.

Turning to face me, she lets out a burst of cynical laughter. "I wanted proof, but this…" shaking her head, she seems to get lost in a moment of despair.

A knock at her door makes both of our eyes snap toward it, but I move first to open it.

Kingsley tries to smile through her worry as she says, "Preston is here."

I immediately walk out to meet him and say, "Tell me everything."

"Yes, Sir." Preston adjusts his glasses on his nose, then unlocks his phone's screen, "I made a video in case we need it." He comes to stand next to me, and I watch as Preston moves through the suite, pointing to a plug, then to the fire alarm. As he continues to point out two more cameras, a sickening feeling grows in my stomach. "There were four in total. I haven't taken them down yet."

"So, they're still active?" I ask.

"Yes, Sir."

"Give me the keycard to the suite."

Preston quickly hands the card over. I walk out of the suite and not having the patience to wait for the elevator, I rush down the stairs. Entering Jamie's old suite, I move closer to the fire alarm.

Staring at the object, rage begins to bubble in my chest.

"I hope you can hear me," I grind the words out. "You're a coward for preying on women. I'm going to find you."

Glaring at the sensor, I wish I could strangle the psycho.

"I'm going to fucking find you, and then I'll destroy you. You chose the wrong girl."

Feeling blinded by rage, I wish I could yank the bastard right through the camera and kill him with my bare hands.

"Julian?" Hearing Jamie behind me, I swing around and jogging over to where she's standing in the doorway, I push her back before shutting the door behind me.

"Don't go in there until they've been taken down. I don't want him seeing you."

"That makes two of us," she mumbles. "Mason called. He's on his way to meet me here. He's called the police, and they should arrive at any moment now."

Just then, the elevator doors open, and two men step out. "Mason Chargill?" They ask as they near us, taking out their badges to identify themselves.

"I'm Julian Reyes. Mason will be here shortly," I explain.

"I'm Detective Olsen, and this is my partner, Detective O'Neal. You reported an invasion of privacy?"

"Yes, a student has found four hidden cameras in his room. Give me a moment to call him."

Taking hold of Jamie's elbow, I pull her closer to me as I bring up Preston's name on my phone. When he answers, I say, "The police are here. Please come down."

Ending the call, I place my phone inside the inner pocket of my jacket.

"Is this the room?" Detective Olsen asks.

"Yes." Letting go of Jamie, I take the keycard from my pocket, and I swipe it, opening the door for them. Not wanting to leave Jamie and not wanting her in the room, I glance at the elevator and let out a sigh of relief when the doors open, and Preston rushes out. "Will you show the Detectives where the cameras are hidden?"

"Yes, Sir."

The moment he steps inside, I pull the door shut behind him, then turn back to Jamie. Seeing the distressed look on her face, I move closer and place my arm around her shoulders, drawing her into my side.

"Thank you for being here," she whispers, her voice tight with tension.

I press another kiss to the top of her head, which has her looking up at me. "I didn't take you for the protective kind."

"Oh?"

She gives me a grateful smile. "I really appreciate it."

"I know."

She grows quiet and stares at the wall for a couple of minutes. "How long has this person been watching me?"

The elevator doors open. Mason, Falcon, and Lake step out.

Lake is the first one to reach us, pulling Jamie away from me and enveloping her in a hug. "How are you holding up?"

Drawing back, she tries her best to smile. "I'm okay."

"Can you stay with her?" I ask Lake, so I can go into the suite with Mason and Falcon.

"Sure, you go ahead."

"The Detectives are inside with Preston," I tell Mason and Falcon, as I open the door.

Stepping inside the room, my gut tells me this is only the beginning of our nightmare.

I can only hope we find him in time before he does something worse.

Chapter 17

"The hunt just got more exciting."

Jamie

Feeling utterly frustrated because the one lead I had is inconclusive, I begin to chew on my thumbnail.

Kingsley reaches up for my finger, pulling my abused thumb away from my mouth. When I glance at her, she gives me a comforting smile while squeezing my hand.

"So, they think the cameras could've been placed while Kingsley was staying in that suite?" Layla asks. "Do you think Serena or Clare would do that?"

"I wouldn't put it past them. They did try to kill us," Kingsley says.

"I wish there was a way to know when the cameras were planted in the room," Falcon murmurs.

"The security team will have to sweep every room on campus. We can't risk assuming anything at this point," Julian adds.

"I'll make the call." Mason gets up and walks out onto the balcony as he pulls out his phone.

"So, we're back to square one," I mutter. It feels like I'm stuck on a rollercoaster ride of terror and despair.

"The police are still investigating it," Julian tries to offer some hope. "Let's wait to see what they come back with."

"Have you eaten today?" Layla asks.

I shake my head, giving her a small smile. "I have zero appetite."

"You should eat, even if it's something small. Want some candy?" Kingsley asks.

"No, thanks. I'll just have one of my smoothies."

Getting up, I go to grab a bottle from the mini-fridge in my room. I take a couple of sips when Julian comes to stand in the doorway.

"Seeing as I'm here, do you want to go to the studio?"

A smile slowly forms around my mouth. "I'll probably suck tonight, but the distraction will be nice."

Not wanting to take the smoothie with me, I drink another huge gulp before I place it back in the fridge.

"Let's go."

I wave at our friends and get a wink from Kingsley and a chuckle from Lake as we walk out of the suite.

"You do know giving me piano lessons is only making them all speculate," I say as we get to the elevator.

"Right now, I couldn't care less." Julian waits for me to step inside before he follows.

Smiling at Julian, I take in the stubble on his jaw, and how tired he looks from the day's events. He's wearing a tan suit with a black dress shirt. "You look nice," I offer a compliment. "Weird how the stubble makes you look even more like a CEO."

The corner of his mouth lifts in a sexy grin. "Not badass?"

I shake my head, and as the doors slide open, I step out and tease, "Nah, you're not badass at all. You're more the dark and broody type."

My comment draws a chuckle from Julian, which has me adding, "You should definitely laugh more, though."

Feeling hot, I wave a hand in front of my face. "I don't know how you can stand the heat with a jacket on."

"I feel fine. Are you hot?" he asks.

"Of course, I'm hot," I joke. "You should know."

It draws another chuckle from him, but then I stumble, and it wipes the smile from Julian's face.

Julian instantly stops walking, and grabbing hold of my shoulders, he leans a little down, inspecting my face with worried eyes. "How do you feel?"

"Just hot." I frown and take a deep breath. "A little dizzy."

I lock eyes with Julian as dread slithers up my spine. When his face becomes blurry, I mumble, "Crap. I think… it's the smoothie."

My legs start to feel wobbly, and I grab hold of Julian's arm.

"I'm taking you to the hospital. I want them to test you right now while it's still in your system," he says, his voice sounding low and dark with concern.

"Please." Anxiety and terror send shockwaves through my body.

I only manage a couple of steps when an intense wave of dizziness hits. Julian grabs hold of me, and when he picks me up to his chest, I don't argue. Wrapping my arms around his neck, I bury my face against his cool skin and feeling scared like never before, I whisper, "Don't leave me alone while I'm passed out."

"Not a chance of that happening." When we reach the car, he helps me stand on my feet, and keeping me pressed to his chest, he quickly opens a door, then helps me into the seat.

With blurring vision, I watch him jog around the car.

My limbs begin to feel heavy as he slides in behind the steering wheel. Feeling horribly vulnerable, I can only manage to slur, "Don't… leave… me… alone."

"I won't."

My eyes drift shut, and it feels like I'm having an out of body experience. I can feel the car move. I can hear Julian's breaths. But I can't move a muscle.

So weird. So scary.

Losing control of my body makes panic crawl into every inch of my being. I've never felt so unsafe before, knowing I'm unable to protect myself from the danger closing in on me.

I begin to drift in and out of consciousness, and at some point, I feel Julian's breath on my forehead as he presses a kiss to my clammy skin. "I'm here. You're safe, Jamie."

Chapter 18

Julian

After Jamie has been placed in the private room, a nurse draws blood, as per my request.

The moment the nurse leaves, I take a seat on the chair next to the bed. I first pull my phone from my pocket before I take hold of Jamie's hand.

Even though she's out cold, I say, "They're going to test for drugs. Rest while we wait for the results."

Bringing up Mason's number, I press dial.

"Miss me already? He answers.

"Are you still at the suite with Kingsley?" I ask.

"Yeah, why?"

"You need to call the police. Have them look at the smoothies Jamie keeps in the mini-fridge in her room. I'm at the hospital with her. She has definitely been drugged, and it can only be from the smoothies she's been drinking."

"What the fuck?" I hear him move, and a second later, he says, "There are two smoothies and a couple of fruit cups inside the fridge."

"Have them clear out everything Jamie has in that fridge. I want it all tested."

"I'll take care of it and then come over to the hospital."

Cutting the call, I go back to my contact list and scroll to Carter's number.

As he answers, I hear him clear his throat before he answers softly, "Carter speaking."

Checking the time and seeing it's past ten here, which means it's already one am in New York, I say, "Sorry for waking you. It's Julian. I'm with Jamie. She's been hospitalized again. I've already requested a drug screen."

"Hold on." I hear him move, probably going to a room where he can talk. A moment later, he says, "What the fuck is going on at Trinity? You promised to keep Jamie safe."

Understanding his anger, I explain, "I was with her when she became drugged. Under the circumstances, I'm keeping her as safe as possible."

"I'll be there in a couple of hours," he bites out. "Don't leave her side until I get there."

"I won't."

The call cuts and I let out an exhausted sigh. I can't blame Carter for being pissed off.

Setting my phone down on the table beside the bed, I bring my hand to Jamie's face and tuck a couple of wild curls behind her ear.

I'm not used to feeling fear and struggle to deal with the emotion as it digs its claws into my heart.

When Jennifer died, the shock knocked me from my feet. There was no fear, only utter desolation.

With Jamie, it's different. It feels like my hands are tied while I watch her slip through my fingers. Someone is trying to hurt her, and I don't know where to begin to find him.

My eyes drift over her face as my thoughts scramble to find a solution to this impossible nightmare.

One thing's for sure – I'll do everything in my power to protect her from the bastard.

He'll have to come through me to get to her.

Unable to tear my eyes away from her face, I finally admit the truth to myself.

I care about Jamie.

More than a one-night-stand.

More than a friend.

No matter how much I try to deny it and use our age gap as a barrier to hide behind, the simple truth is that I care a hell of a lot about this woman.

Needing to express what I'm feeling, I whisper, "It meant something to me." Caressing her features with my gaze, I admit, "The night we spent together meant more to me than you'll ever know."

Minutes after my confession, the door opens, and Mason walks in, followed by Lake and Falcon.

"How is she?" Lake asks, instantly moving to the other side of the bed. He gives her free hand a squeeze, concern etched deep on his face.

The man has a heart the size of Texas, and I love him for it.

"She's sleeping. I think it will take a while before the drug works out of her system." Looking at Mason, I ask, "Did the police take the smoothies?"

"Yes, they said they would send it to a crime lab for testing," Mason replies while shooting a worried glance at Jamie.

Falcon comes to stand next to me, and placing his hand on my shoulder, he says, "She'll be fine."

I shake my head. "How can she be with all the shit happening to her?" I let out a harsh breath. "And the bastard is still out there. Who knows when he'll strike again?" I glance up at Falcon. "Hire a team of guards. The best there is. I want them guarding Jamie twenty-four-seven."

"Yes, that would be best. We can't leave her alone now, not with her in so much danger."

Falcon gives my shoulder a squeeze, which has me reaching up and placing my hand over his.

"Thank you for being here," I whisper.

"Always."

After a moment, Lake asks, "Can I go get you some coffee?"

"That would be nice."

"I need some too," Mason says, then he glances at Falcon, "Do you want coffee?"

Yes, please." Falcon waits for Lake to leave, then he says, "You care about her."

I nod, not hiding the truth from my brother.

"Do you know how she feels about you?"

I let out a chuckle. "I'm not sure. It constantly changes from hating my guts to giving me a hard time."

My comment draws a burst of soft laughter from Falcon. "She cares then, or she'd just ignore your stubborn ass."

"Even if she does, it doesn't mean we can be in a relationship," I voice my concern.

"Why not?" Falcon pulls another chair closer and takes a seat next to me.

"She's our biggest partner's sister-in-law." I take a deep breath and add, "Carter is on his way, and he's pissed off."

"We'll handle it when he gets here." Falcon tilts his head to the side, his eyes locking with mine. "I would think with her being Carter's family, it would actually solidify the partnership if you and Jamie got together."

"And if things don't work out between us?"

Falcon shrugs. "Then it doesn't work out, but at least you would've tried, right?" Leaning a little forward, a serious look settles on his features. "Besides, you're stable, and once you commit, there's no stopping you. As long as Jamie is in one hundred percent, I can't see why a relationship won't work between the two of you."

My eyes drift back to Jamie's face as I think over Falcon's words.

"It doesn't matter right now. First, we need to eliminate the threat to her life."

"We will." Falcon lets out a deep breath, then murmurs, "Somehow, we will."

After a moment of silence, Falcon reaches over and places his hand on my arm. "As long as you know, I'm here for you."

"Thank you." A tired but grateful smile forms around my mouth. "I get a feeling I'm going to need you now more than ever."

Falcon gives me a comforting smile, then he changes the subject. "Have you seen Dad lately?"

"No." I take a deep breath before admitting, "I've been avoiding him because the second he finds out about what's been happening, he will lose his shit, and I don't want to be in the line of fire."

"He's going to find out sooner rather than later, and that will only make him angrier," Falcon warns.

"You're right, but I'm not going to worry about it now. I'll deal with it once I know Jamie is safe."

"Just give me a heads up before you tell him so I can flee the country," Falcon jokes.

—————————————

The moment Carter bursts through the door, I rise from the chair.

His features are tight with anger and worry, and he first walks over to Jamie, inspecting her sleeping face and pressing a kiss to her forehead before turning to me.

"What the hell is going on at Trinity?"

"We've brought in the police after we found hidden cameras in her old suite, but there's no way of knowing for sure whether they were placed in the room before or after she moved in. I'm arranging private guards for Jamie. Right now, the hospital is running tests. The police have also sent what's left of the smoothies Jamie drinks for testing." I tell Carter everything I know.

Crossing his arms over his chest, he shakes his head as he looks down at Jamie again. "The minute she wakes up, I'm taking her home."

His words shouldn't surprise me, but they do.

Not liking the idea of being separated from Jamie, I say, "That might not solve the problem. If this person is serious about hurting Jamie, they might just follow her to New York."

There's a painful look of frustration on Carter's face. "How many guards will she have?"

"As many as it takes to keep her safe," I answer. All I want to do is lock her in a room until we've dealt with the bastard, but that would be insane.

165

Carter seems to think about something, then says, "Rhett's father-in-law is a retired Navy Seal. I'm going to give him a call and ask for help because I don't trust the police to catch this psycho in time. Hayden and his teammate, Max, have dealt with situations like this one before."

I'm caught by surprise and feel a slither of relief. "That would help a hell of a lot."

I watch as Carter pulls out his phone and dials a number, then he says, "Hey, Rhett. Sorry, I know it's late. Jamie's been drugged again. I'm at the hospital. Can you do me a favor and give Hayden a call? Ask whether he and Max can lend us a hand?"

Carter listens for a moment, then replies, "Thanks. I appreciate it. I'll keep you up to date if anything happens here."

As he cuts the call, movement from Jamie has us both stepping forward. When she opens her eyes, she blinks up at us a couple of times before glancing around the room.

Confusion masks her face for a moment before panic tightens her features. "What happened?" Pain flashes in her eyes as she slowly sits up.

"How are you feeling?" I ask, wanting to know if I should call a nurse.

"It feels like I have one hell of a hangover." She looks from Carter to me, then asks, "It happened again, didn't it?"

"What's the last thing you remember from last night? I ask.

She thinks a little, and bringing her hand to her face, she rubs her eyes. "Ah... we were sitting in the living room."

"You had a smoothie, and on the way to the studio for a piano lesson, you started to show symptoms of being drugged," I bring her up to date. "I brought you to the hospital so they could test you immediately."

I watch as fear darkens the blue of her eyes and not caring that Carter is here, I sit down on the bed and hug her to me, and wanting to offer her some sense of security, I say, "I didn't leave you alone for a second. You were safe the entire night."

Wrapping her arms around my neck, she holds me tightly and whispers, "Thank you."

When I pull back, I lift my hands and frame her face. "I'm arranging private security for you. Until they arrive, I think you should stay in the hotel with me."

Surprise flickers in her eyes before she glances up at Carter, who I momentarily forgot about.

167

"There are two rooms in the penthouse," I quickly add when Carter glances between Jamie and me.

"Oh, good," he states. "Then you won't mind if I stay a couple of days."

Fuck.

Carter locks eyes with me, and I see the warning clear as daylight, then his voice rumbles low, "You better not think of screwing my sister-in-law."

"Carter!" Jamie exclaims.

Well, it's a little late for that.

Getting up, I square my shoulders. "Carter, if something were to happen between Jamie and me, it wouldn't be a mere fling."

He lifts his chin, his eyes boring into mine. "Outside."

"Carter, stop!" Jamie gasps.

I place my hand on her shoulder and give her a comforting squeeze. "Don't worry. I'll handle this. Get some more rest."

"Like hell," she snaps. "If you're going to talk about me, you're doing it right here."

"Fine," Carter growls and coming to stand in front of me, he asks, "Are you interested in Jamie?"

It's a simple question for which I don't have a clear answer. "With everything that's happening right now, it's

168

hard to think of romance, Carter." He clenches his jaw, and not wanting this to escalate, I answer honestly, "Jamie is amazing, beautiful, smart, and funny. Of course, I'm interested in her, but right now, it's the last thing on my mind. Once she's safe, we can talk again."

Carter takes a deep breath, calming down a little.

Wanting to ease his mind some more, I add, "I take a relationship seriously, so if I were to ever start one with Jamie, it would be for the long haul."

"Well, that's good to know," Jamie says drily. "Can we turn down the testosterone levels now? You're both making my headache worse."

Carter shakes his head, and a hopeless look flashes over his face. "Sorry, I didn't mean to get aggressive. It's just…"

"I understand. I feel frustrated, as well." I give him an encouraging smile, then I offer, "If you're sticking around for a couple of days, we could stay at my family home."

"That would be great. Della and the kids can join us for the weekend."

"Do I get a say?" Jamie asks, glaring at both of us.

"Of course," Carter smiles at her. "Do you want to pack your things and come back to New York or…"

Before he can finish the sentence, Jamie interrupts with, "Nope. I'm good with visiting Julian's family home."

"Then it's settled." Grabbing my phone from next to the bed, I tuck it in my inner pocket.

"Where are you going?" Jamie asks, her eyes resting intensely on me.

"I'm just going to check in with Mason. I'll be back in thirty minutes." Leaning over her, I press a kiss to her forehead, then nod my head at Carter before I leave the room.

Well, that went better than I anticipated.

Chapter 19

Jamie

Standing by the window in the living room, I watch as Mr. Reyes, Julian, and Carter talk with the security guards Julian brought in for my protection.

"There are always two of you by her side, unless Mr. Hayes or myself is with her," Julian instructs.

Mr. Reyes, Julian's father, walks to where I'm standing. "Would you like to take a walk with me, Miss Truman?"

A smile stretches across my face. "I'd like that very much."

Resting my arm in the crook of his, we walk out of the house. The grounds surrounding the mansion are gorgeous.

"You have a beautiful home," I compliment him.

"Thank you, dear." We walk toward a bench under an old oak tree, and once we're seated, Mr. Reyes says, "I hope Julian has been treating you well."

"He has. I'm extremely grateful for his support."

Mr. Reyes turns his eyes to me, and for a while, he just stares. "How are you really doing?"

"I'd be lying if I said I'm not scared," I admit.

"You're welcome to stay here for as long as you like." He gives me a warm smile, and hearing the kindness in his voice suddenly makes me want to cry. "Would it be preposterous of an old man to offer you a comforting hug?"

I shake my head as my chin starts to tremble.

Mr. Reyes opens his arms, and I don't need a second invitation. Resting my head on his shoulder, his arms form bands of security around me. For a moment, I feel safe, and it seems as if nothing can harm me.

Having never known my father, I wonder if he would've been as caring as Mr. Reyes. He looks like an older version of his sons, his shoulders square with pride, and his eyes sharp with intelligence.

"All feels lost when we're faced with the horrors hidden in the dark corners of life," he murmurs. "But you're not alone, Miss Truman. My family and I will raise an army and go to war on your behalf. You just stay here and rest your battle-weary heart."

Feeling emotional because I'm getting a taste of what it's like to have a father for the first time in my life, I struggle to hold the tears in.

Lifting my head, I press a kiss to his cheek before I wrap my arms around his neck and hug him tightly. "Thank you so much."

Drawing back, I say, "Julian and Falcon are lucky to have you."

Mr. Reyes lifts a hand to my cheek, wiping a tear away. "Since I've retired, I have a lot of idle time. Why don't you do me a favor and tell me more about yourself?"

"You might regret asking," I tease. "Once I start talking, it's hard to make me stop."

When Mr. Reyes crosses a leg over the other and leans back.

I settle in, as well. "I have an older sister, Della. She's married to Carter. I helped raise my niece the first four years of her life," I tell him with pride because Danny has turned into a beautiful little girl. "We grew up in Saluda, it's a small town in North Carolina."

When I pause for a moment, Mr. Reyes asks, "Do your parents still live there?"

Swallowing hard because I still feel overly emotional, I say, "My father passed away a couple of months before I was born, and my mother was taken by cancer when I was six."

"Loss is a terrible thing," Mr. Reyes whispers. "We never fully recover from the blow it deals us."

"Yeah," I agree, remembering I said something similar to Julian the other night at dinner.

"I understand you're studying law?" he asks, changing the subject from my parents.

"Yes, I like arguing," I joke.

Mr. Reyes lets out a deep chuckle, then his eyes rest on Julian, where he's standing on the porch with Carter. Every now and then, Julian glances at us.

"My son takes after me, Miss Truman. He can be stubborn as a mule, but he's loyal to a fault."

"I won't argue about that," I laugh.

"He also loves deeply," Mr. Reyes continues and realizing where this conversation is going, it wipes the smile from my face. "It broke his heart when his fiancée passed away, and you're the first woman who's company I've seen him enjoy since."

My eyes drift to Julian, remembering what he said to Carter about if we were ever to start a relationship.

'Jamie is amazing, beautiful, smart, and funny. Of course, I'm interested in her, but right now, it's the last thing on my mind.'

"Be gentle with my son, Miss Truman. Even though he's stronger than I ever was, I'm not sure he'll survive heartbreak a second time."

Turning my gaze back to Mr. Reyes, I see the worry on his face. "I'll do everything in my power to not hurt him." I take a deep breath as I let my gaze wander back to Julian and Carter.

If anything goes wrong and I'm faced with death, I'll fight with everything I have.

The thought is a terrifying one, and it steals my breath for a moment. My heart begins to race at the mere notion of coming face to face with whoever's been stalking me.

I'll fight for Della because I know she can't lose me as well.

Mr. Reyes places his hand on my back, and it makes tears blur my vision as I watch Julian and Carter walk our way.

I'm surrounded by the most powerful families in America, yet I feel utterly powerless.

How do you survive an onslaught from someone who doesn't care about who you are and has no respect for human life?

I walk to the kitchen to get a glass of water and hear the footsteps right behind me. It's going to take some getting used to being followed by guards all the time.

Opening the cupboard where the glasses are, I turn to the two guards, and ask, "Can I get y'all water?"

They both nod, and as I take three glasses from the shelf, Carter calls from deeper in the house, "Jamie!"

"In the kitchen," I shout back.

He comes jogging into the room. "Miss Sebastian is on the line."

Taking his phone, I bring it to my ear. "Hey, Miss Sebastian."

"Angel-child." Her voice is void of its usual cheerfulness. "The toxicology report we did on your hair strands came back. It tested positive for gamma-hydroxybutyrate. It's a central nervous system depressant better known as GHB." She takes a deep breath, then says, "Jamie, you were roofied."

Shocked from the news, I stare at Carter.

"Are you there, Jamie?"

"Yeah, I'm just a little…" I thought I'd be relieved to hear I'm not losing my mind, but I'm not. I'm terrified.

Carter takes the phone from me, and I vaguely hear him talk with Miss Sebastian as I slowly walk out of the kitchen.

I reach the library, and my eyes land on Julian, where he's working at a desk. Walking closer to him, his head snaps up. Rising from the chair, he asks, "What's wrong? Did something happen?"

"The test came back positive," I whisper. Closing the distance between us, I wrap my arms around his waist and bury my face in his chest. "I was drugged."

Julian doesn't hesitate, and when I feel his arms around me, realization hits.

Julian's arms were the ones I wanted to feel.

"I'm not going to let anything happen to you," he says.

Julian's words were the ones I wanted to hear.

Pulling back, I look up at the face of the man I've fallen for.

'I'm not sure he'll survive heartbreak a second time.'

Remembering Mr. Reyes' words, I take a step away from Julian, and then another.

"Ah... I should go talk to Carter."

Turning around, I rush out of the room, and when I get to my bedroom, I slam the door shut before the guards can follow me inside.

I don't know what scares me more, falling for Julian, or knowing there's a person out there who can end my life before I've even had a chance to feel what it's like to love a man.

Chapter 20

Julian

When both tests came back positive for GHB, the police came to interview Jamie again, this time asking about previous boyfriends, and whether she can think of anyone who would want to harm her.

I can see she's shaken up by the interview because she's been quieter since we got the results, and the police left.

I walk into the living room, where Jamie is sitting on the couch, lost in her thoughts. Taking a seat next to her, I place my hand on her leg. "Want to talk about it?"

She gets up and gives me a forced, polite smile. "I'm tired of talking about it. I want to go back to Trinity. I'm missing too many classes."

After dropping the bomb, she rushes out of the room, leaving me confused.

What's going on?

I get up and go after her. "Jamie, hold up."

She keeps walking, saying, "I need to talk to Carter."

I follow her into Carter's room and watch as she stares at him until he ends the call he's on. "I want to go back to Trinity. I can't stay here forever."

"Jamie…" Carter begins.

"It's not open for discussion," she says, then rushing by me, she leaves the room.

Carter turns his eyes to me, looking as confused as I feel, "What happened?"

"I have no idea. This is news to me, as well."

"We better stop her," he says. We walk to Jamie's room and see the two guards standing by her closed door.

"Take a break," I say, wanting privacy for what's sure to be an argument.

Carter knocks on the door before he enters. When I step inside, I watch as Jamie throws clothes into a bag.

"Can you stop for a moment?" Carter asks.

"Nope. I'm in a hurry. I have a lot of work to catch up on," she says without looking at us.

"Della is coming tomorrow, Jamie. It's Friday. Why would you want to go back right now?"

She closes the bag, then finally turns to look at Carter. "I'm done hiding, Carter. I'm no safer here than I'll be at

Trinity. Changing my address is not going to stop that creep from coming after me."

"You are safer here," I argue.

Jamie first glances down and takes a deep breath before she brings her eyes to me. "I'm not going to put my life on hold. If I do that, the creep wins." She moves her gaze to Carter. "I'll come to visit Della and the kids, but I'm going back to Trinity today. I also want my own suite. Now that I have guards, I don't have to stay with Layla and Kingsley any longer."

What the fuck?

Where is this coming from?

Jamie

"Can I have a moment alone with Jamie?" Carter asks Julian.

I can see he's reluctant to leave, but he does as Carter asks.

Once we're alone, Carter comes over to me and takes hold of my shoulders. "Now, tell me what's really going on."

I shake my head and look down when the act I've worked so hard to put on, becomes too much to bear.

Carter leans a little down to catch my eyes. "Talk to me."

"I'm terrified," I say, harsher than I meant to. "I'm so terrified. What if this person hurts someone I care about because he can't get to me? What if... " My breaths come faster, and I cover my mouth to keep the sob back.

Carter brings his hands up and framing my face, he gives me an intense look. "So, you thought it would be better to separate yourself from everyone? Did you actually think we'd allow you to do that?" Pulling me to his chest, he wraps me in a tight hug. "You've always been the one who took care of us. Let me take care of you now."

Pulling back, I shake my head. "I can't, Carter. Della needs you. Danny and Christopher need you. Y'all have to go back to New York."

I glance down at the bandage around my arm. I can barely look at the cut whenever I have to clean it.

"Some creep drugged me multiple times. He was in my suite, and I'm sure the cameras were planted by him. He has already tried to kill me once." Bringing my eyes back to Carter, I shake my head as hopelessness threatens to engulf me. "He's never going to stop. It feels like a shadow is following me around."

"All the more reason for you to stay here," Carter argues. "Hayden and Max will be here soon. With them helping, I'm sure we'll catch the guy in no time."

"I'm glad they're coming, but do you think I'll be able to live with myself if something happened to you, or to Julian, or to Mr. Reyes? What if something happens to Della because she came out here? You need to tell her to stay in New York."

I can see my words are starting to get through to Carter, and it makes me push harder. "Tristan can not grow up never having known his father. Your family should come first, Carter."

"You are my family!" Turning away from me, he rubs a hand over his face. "Fuck!" When he turns back to me, his eyes are shimmering with unshed tears, and it kills me to see him so upset. "I can't just leave you behind, Jamie. Now more than ever, we need to stand together."

"What if he kills you?" I shout, my emotions overwhelming me. My legs give way, and I sink to the floor as a cry rips through me. "What if he kills me?"

Carter drops to his knees in front of me and frames my face. "That's not going to happen."

"You don't know that." I gasp for air, and wrapping my arms around his neck, I beg, "Please go home. I need you to be safe in New York with Della and the kids. I'm going to lose my mind with worry if you stay here."

Carter holds me so tightly it's bordering on painful. His voice is hoarse as he says, "Don't ask me to leave, Jamie."

Julian

The last couple of hours have been an emotional rollercoaster. Carter managed to calm Jamie down and talked her into staying at the mansion until Sunday.

Leaning against the pillar where I'm standing on the porch, I watch Jamie sitting on a bench in the garden.

"You should go talk with her," Dad says as he comes outside with two cups of coffee. "Take one to Miss Truman."

Taking the cups from him, I smile. "Thanks, Dad."

I walk down the stairs, and when I reach the bench, Jamie doesn't even look up.

"My dad sends coffee," I say, holding a cup to her.

She takes the coffee, then stares down at it.

"You're really not going to talk to me?" I ask before I take a sip of the warm liquid.

"What do you want me to say?" she asks, her voice sounding empty of all emotion.

"Whatever's on your mind."

Her head snaps up, and she gives me an angry look. "Really? Do you really want me to tell you what I'm thinking?"

Taking the cup from her, I place it on the ground, along with my own. "Yes, I want you to *really* tell me *exactly* what you're thinking."

She gets up and walks a couple of steps away, then turning back to me, she shouts, "I'm terrified out of my mind."

I get up and walk two steps closer. "Should I get more security?"

"No, Julian! I'm scared for Della, and Danny and Christopher, and Carter." She fists her hands at her sides as her breaths speed up. "I'm scared for you." Her shoulders slump under the fear. "What if the person comes after someone I care about?"

I stare at her as her words sink in. She just placed me in the same bracket as her family.

Does that mean…?

I close the distance between us and wrap my arms around her.

How do you comfort someone when there is no certainty that none of their fears won't come true?

You lie.

"We're going to get through this. We have more security than the president."

Jamie pulls back, and I can see my words have done nothing to ease her fears.

Framing her face, I press my forehead to hers. "We're going to get through this, and then we're going to go on a date. When we agree the time is right, we'll spend a night together, and you'll still be there when I wake up. We'll learn each other's faults. We're going to get through this together because we both have something to lose."

Jamie closes her eyes as tears roll down her cheeks. "I can't do that to you, Julian."

When she opens her eyes again, there's so much heartache in them. It guts me to see her like this.

She pulls away and wipes her cheeks, then first takes a couple of deep breaths before, she says, "You can't go through that pain again."

Chapter 21

Where are you hiding, beautiful?

Jamie

Julian tilts his head to the side, his eyes boring into mine.

"Again?" he says, his voice too calm for the anger I see coming to life on his face. "Have you already decided you're going to die?"

My frustration only grows because I can't make any of them understand. "No, but let's be real for a second. There's a crazy person out there who has tried to kill me before. We have nothing. No clues to who it could be. The odds aren't exactly in my favor."

Julian gestures to the house. "The odds aren't in your favor? How do you figure that? I have a small army guarding you! I'd say the fucker is greatly outnumbered."

"For how long? What if this person is never found?"

"Then you'll have to get used to living with protection."

"It's that easy?" I ask, my fight draining from me. I'm exhausted to my core. "I can't live like a prisoner, Julian."

For a moment, he closes his eyes as he tries to remain calm. "You won't be the first person to have guards. Unfortunately, when you're a member of certain families, it comes with the territory."

I hear what he's saying. "Fine, but I'm still going back to school. I can't just sit around and wait for him to strike."

"On Sunday, after dinner, I'll take you myself."

"Will you get guards for yourself as well?" I ask.

"Will it make you feel better if I arrange security for everyone?" he asks, the anger fading from his voice.

"It will make me feel a hell of a lot better."

"Then, consider it done."

"Really?" I ask to make sure.

"Jamie," he moves closer to me, and pulling me back against his chest, continues, "I'll do whatever it takes to make you feel safe. If that means starting a security company of my own, then so be it."

I let out a chuckle, and rest my cheek against his beating heart. "Thank you."

Julian

When we sit down for dinner, I forgo the head of the table and take the seat next to Jamie.

Dad walks into the dining room and pauses when he sees me next to Jamie. "Oh, good, good."

I suppress a chuckle when he goes to sit at the head with a smile on his face. Stephanie takes the seat next to him.

"It's so good to have everyone here," Dad says, and lifting his glass of wine, he toasts, "To family and new friends."

When the servers bring out the food, Dad asks, "Carter, how's the publishing business?"

"It's good, Sir. We've just opened a translation department and hope to break into the European market."

Dad and Carter get absorbed in talking business, which has Stephanie asking, "Della, when are you due?"

"In four weeks."

"Oh, wow, it's right around the corner." Stephanie smiles, then asks, "Do you know the sex yet?"

"We're having another boy. We've decided to name him Tristan."

"It's a beautiful name," Stephanie compliments her.

While we enjoy the entrée, I notice Jamie's leg jumping. Moving my left hand under the table, I place it on her thigh, which makes the jumping instantly stop.

The dishes are cleared, and when soup bowls are placed in front of us, Jamie slips her hand under the table and taking hold of mine, she turns it over before weaving her fingers through mine.

"Can you eat with just your left hand?" I ask softly, so the others won't hear.

"We'll find out soon enough," she jokes.

Dinner is relaxing, and for a moment, I manage to forget about everything.

Jamie

Tomorrow Hayden and Max will come to see if they can help. I have only met them twice, but from what I remember, they looked pretty badass, so it feels like there might be a glimmer of hope in this nightmare.

Not being able to sleep, I climb out of bed and walk to the kitchen. Switching on a light, I pour myself a glass of water, then lean back against a counter and take a sip.

I'm deep in thought when Julian walks into the kitchen. He's only wearing sweatpants, and the moment my eyes focus on his bare chest and abs, I spew the water all over the kitchen floor, then choke when a couple of drops go down the wrong hole.

"I didn't know you were up," he says as he grabs a couple of paper towels.

Clearing my throat to get rid of the burn, I place the glass in the sink, then crouch to help him wipe up the mess.

"You could wear a shirt, you know," I say, my voice hoarse from choking on water.

Yep, it's definitely not hoarse because I have a close-up view of his abs.

"You could wear pants," he shoots back as he goes to throw the paper towels in the trash can.

Climbing to my feet, I yank my oversized shirt up and say, "I'm wearing pants."

Julian's eyes drop down to my pelvic area, and then his eyebrow lifts. "You call those pants?"

"Yeah." I glance down at my shorts. Sure, they're a little tight, but they're one of my comfy pairs.

A sexy smirk begins to form around Julian's mouth, which instantly has me frowning. "What's the grin for?"

He slowly moves closer to me, then says, "You choked when you saw me. I'm just wondering why."

"Don't let it go to your head," I taunt him. "It's nothing I haven't seen before."

"Yeah, and if memory serves me right, you really liked the view the first time around."

And what a view it was, seeing him in all his naked glory.

I begin to feel flushed from the memory of our night together and having him standing so close to me.

Clearing my throat again, I do my best to keep my eyes on his face because one more look at his chest might have me drooling.

Julian tilts his head and takes another step closer, which has our bodies almost touching. It's close enough for me to feel the heat of his skin.

My eyes jump to his chest before bringing them back to his face. When I see his irises darkening with the same desire that's spreading through me like a fire, I forget that we're standing in the kitchen.

"This is a bad idea," he murmurs as he lifts a hand to the back of my neck.

"Yeah," I agree, my breaths already speeding up with anticipation.

His other hand clamps down on my hip, and as he pulls me closer, he lowers his head to mine. The moment our lips touch, I bring up my hands to frame his jaw.

I'm overwhelmed by his scent, something citrusy, which is probably from the body wash he uses. Feeling his chest press against mine, my body shudders, and I move my hands to his hair.

Julian nips at my bottom lip, and it makes my heart rate spike. I part my lips, and his tongue immediately sweeps into my mouth, drawing a needy moan from me.

When Julian slips a hand up the back of my shirt, and his fingers brush over my sensitive skin, I push my body hard against his, wanting so much more.

"Oh shit," I hear Della's surprised voice.

Julian instantly breaks the kiss, and we both glance at the entrance to the kitchen, but Della's nowhere to be found, probably having rushed away to give us privacy.

Julian lets out a chuckle and dropping his head, he presses a kiss to my neck, then whispers, "Busted."

"Yep. I better go after her and explain." Reluctantly, I pull away from Julian.

"What are you going to say to her?" Julian asks, his eyes still resting on me filled with intense desire.

"The truth." I drop my eyes only for them to land on his golden skin.

"And that is?" he asks as he lifts a hand to my jaw, and then rubs his thumb softly over my bottom lip.

Holy cow, if he doesn't stop, I'm going to forget about wanting to talk with Della and drag him back to my room.

"We... ah... spent a night together," I stumble over my words because all brain activity is solely focused on Julian, and how he's making me feel. "That the kiss just happened... and I'm not sure... what it means."

Julian moves his hand down to the side of my neck, and then he leans in and presses a soft kiss to my lips. Pulling back, his eyes find mine. "Hopefully, it means there's still a mutual attraction, and we'd both like to see where it will lead?"

I begin to nod and agree, "I'll tell Della that. It's less complicated."

The corner of Julian's mouth lifts. "When you're done talking with your sister, and you can't sleep, come to my room."

My eyebrow pops up, not having expected the offer even after we just shared a hot kiss.

My reaction has Julian saying, "To sleep, Jamie. Just to sleep. Let's take it slow this time."

I smile, appreciating that he's willing to move slow. Walking toward the entrance of the kitchen, I warn him, "You might regret the invitation because I'm a restless sleeper."

Chapter 22

Julian

Staring out of my window at the dark night, I replay what just happened over in my mind.

For a moment, I doubt myself, wondering if I made a mistake kissing Jamie.

It felt right, though.

Why hold off until the perpetrator is caught? It might take months.

I'm done fighting the attraction I feel for Jamie. Yes, she's much younger than me, but she's like no other woman I've ever met. She challenges me, never backing away from an argument.

There's a soft knock at my door, and when I glance over my shoulder, Jamie pushes the door open.

"Does the offer still stand?"

Seeing the unsure look on her face, I turn around and gesture at the bed. "Of course."

She steps inside the room and shuts the door before she glances at the bed. "Just to sleep, right?"

A smile tugs at my mouth. "Just to sleep."

Walking to the bed, I sit down on the right-hand side as it's closest to the door. Stretching my legs out, I grin when Jamie slowly inches her way closer, and giving me one last look, she pulls the covers back and climbs inside.

Snuggling into a pillow, she mutters, "I'm probably not going to sleep."

I lean over her and switch off the lamp on the nightstand. Drawing back, I hear her exhale a deep breath.

Making myself comfortable, I lie on my back, and it takes a moment for my eyes to adjust to the dark.

"What did Della say?" I ask, curious to know if she approves or whether I have to prepare myself for a backlash.

"She just wanted to know if I'm sure about starting a relationship with you."

Turning onto my side, I look at Jamie. "And? Are you sure?"

Her tongue darts out and she wets her lips, before answering, "To be honest, I haven't thought that far. The kiss was unexpected."

"It was," I agree. "But now that it's happened, how do you feel?"

"I don't regret it." Her eyes search my face. "How do you feel about the kiss?"

I reach out a hand to her and brush some of her hair back. "It felt right."

Our eyes lock, and having her in my bed, makes my need for her rush back.

"And now I regret having said we'll only sleep tonight," I tease her.

"Yeah?" She moves closer. "Why's that?"

Letting out a chuckle, I wrap an arm around her waist and pull her body against mine. "Lift your head." She does as I ask, and I push my arm under her. When she rests her head by my shoulder, I lean closer and press a kiss to her mouth. "Time to sleep."

"You didn't answer my question," she argues.

"I'm not going to." Turning my face to her, I inhale the fresh scent of her hair, then whisper, "Sleep, Jamie."

Holding her tighter against me, a smile plays around my lips.

This feels right.

Jamie

When I wake up, it takes a moment before I realize my face is pressed to Julian's chest, and I'm drooling on him.

I dart up and using the hem of my shirt, I wipe up the patch of drool on his skin before I take a moment to blink the sleep away.

A chuckle from Julian has my eyes snapping to his.

"Morning," he whispers, his voice gravelly from just having woken.

"Morning." Wow, I can't remember when last I slept that well.

I'm not sure if I should leave, so I just stare at him, drinking in how good he looks with his hair tousled and a shadow of a beard forming on his jaw.

"So this is what you look like when you stay the night?" he teases, and it has me reaching up so I can pat my hair down.

Julian takes hold of my arm and pulls me back down. "Give me five more minutes, then you can run away."

Wrapping an arm around his waist, I snuggle into his side.

"Are you always this quiet when you wake up?"

"Uh-huh." I close my eyes and take a deep breath of his scent, the citrus now almost gone.

There's a moment's silence, then Julian says, "You know if you go back to the dorm, you'll have to sleep alone."

I push my upper body up on my arm and look down at him. "Oh, so this wasn't a one-time offer?"

A smile tugs at the corners of his mouth, and his eyes are a softer shade of brown as he stares at me. "Of course, not."

"Mmh… you could always stay at the dorm with me," I tease, knowing he won't because the students will talk.

That's if I'm not already the highlight of the gossip mill.

"I've done my time there," he jokes.

Glancing at the alarm clock next to his bed, I say, "I have to get ready. Hayden and Max are arriving at nine."

Julian's arms come around me, and he pushes me back on the bed. Pressing a quick kiss to my mouth, he suddenly lets me go and climbs out of bed.

I first stare at the sweatpants hanging low on his hips, giving me a perfect view of his V before I scoot over to his side and stand up.

"See you at breakfast."

I begin to walk toward the door, but Julian grabs hold of my hand and playfully yanks me back to him. He brings his other hand to the side of my neck and presses a harder kiss to my lips before letting me go.

I stare at him, loving how affectionate he is. "I could get used to this."

My words make him grin. "That's the idea."

Chapter 23

Jamie

I stand next to Julian as a car pulls up the driveway of the mansion. Rhett arrived thirty minutes earlier, and I watch as he and Carter walk toward the vehicle.

When Hayden and Max climb out and shake hands with Carter and Rhett, I let out a deep breath of relief.

Just seeing the two hardened veterans makes me feel better.

Hayden hangs back to talk with Rhett while Max walks toward me. I notice how his eyes never stop scanning over the surrounding area. Reaching me, his eyes meet mine with an intense look.

The first time I met Max, I couldn't hold eye contact with him, but now I force myself to not look away.

"Jamie, it's good to see you again. Wish it was under better circumstances," he says in a low growl, and it makes the tiny hairs on the back of my neck stand up.

I'd be stupid not to fear this man a little. The things he must've seen and experienced in his life makes my own problems pale in comparison.

For a moment, my eyes drift over the scars on his face. I heard he got them during his last mission.

"Hi, Max." My voice sounds like I'm fourteen again, filled with the unknown fear of having to bury another loved one.

Even though Max's posture is relaxed, his gaze keeps boring into mine. "We'll catch the person."

One sentence. That's all it takes to make the tension snap inside of me.

Not caring that he's a badass Navy Seal, I throw myself forward and wrap my arms around his neck. Max doesn't even budge a muscle from the impact of my body hitting his. He wraps two strong arms around me, and I get the same feeling I had with Mr. Reyes – the safety only a father figure's arms can provide.

"Julian, let me introduce you," I hear Rhett say. "This is Hayden Cole and Max Perry."

I pull away so Max can greet Julian.

"Nice to meet you," Hayden says, shaking hands with Julian, then he turns to me and nods his head at me. "Jamie."

When everyone begins to move inside the house, Hayden takes hold of my elbow and asks Carter and Rhett. "Can Max and I have a moment alone with Jamie?"

"Sure, we'll be in the living room when you're done," Rhett answers his father-in-law.

I can see Julian's not too happy with the idea, and then he says, "There's a bench under the oak tree you can sit and talk."

"Thanks."

I smile at Julian before I lead the two men over the bench, and when I turn to sit down, I notice Julian's still standing on the porch, his eyes never leaving me.

Hayden sits down next to me while Max remains standing, crossing his arms over his broad chest.

"Thanks for coming out here," I say.

"No need to thank us," Max grumbles.

"Is there anything you can tell us? It doesn't matter how insignificant you think it might be," Hayden asks.

I think back over the past couple of weeks. "He had to watch me, to learn that I drink a smoothie at night."

"Did you lock your room whenever you left?" Hayden asks.

"The door automatically locks. I have a keycard to open it."

Hayden looks up at Max. "The person knows how things work around the campus, in order to get into her room. It could be a student or an employee."

"Why me, though?" I ask the million-dollar question.

"Because this person is sick in the head, that's the only real reason," Max answers.

Hearing him say the words offer me some comfort that it's not because of something I did.

Julian

"We'll take over guarding Jamie," Hayden says, his tone offering no option to discuss the matter.

"What about the ranch?" Rhett asks.

"We have people caring for it," Max answers from where he's standing with his back to a wall in the living room, facing all of us.

"And the current guards?" I ask. "Do we keep them to relieve you when you're sleeping?"

Hayden nods before he answers, "We only need four hours sleep."

"Where will you stay?" Jamie asks. Trust her to think about the men while we're discussing her safety.

"I'll have a suite set up for them on the floor beneath yours," I reply.

"Looks like we're going back to school," Max murmurs, which draws a chuckle from Hayden.

Hayden looks at Jamie. "What time are we leaving?"

"After dinner. I already packed everything." Jamie gets up from the sofa then looks at her sister. "Let's go for a walk."

I watch the two women leave, then my eyes go back to Hayden and Max. At first glance, they scared the living shit out of me, but once I spoke with them, the apprehension quickly turned to a sense of comfort.

I'm still not at ease with the idea of Jamie going back to Trinity, though, and I keep watching the two men who will be responsible for her safety.

Hayden must pick up on my unease because he walks toward me. "Is there a room we can talk in private?"

"Sure." I get up and head toward the library.

When Hayden follows me inside, he shuts the door behind us, then bluntly asks, "Are you close with Jamie?"

I meet his unyielding gaze with one of my own. "Yes."

When I don't offer more information, he takes a step closer. "To what degree?"

Feeling that he doesn't need to know every detail about our relationship, I reply, "I care for her."

"We all care for her." He takes another step forward, and it makes the corner of my mouth lift.

"Are you trying to intimidate me right now?"

The harsh lines around his mouth ease away as he smiles. "I need to know whether you'll fight for her or run away if the time comes."

I know he's only doing his job, and I shouldn't take his comment personally, but it still grinds against my gut. "I'll fight for her."

Our eyes remain locked for a moment, then he asks, "Have you ever handled a weapon?"

"I've been hunting with my father since I was thirteen."

"I'm only asking so I know for future reference." He lets out a breath, then walks over to the wall lined with books. Scanning over the novels, he asks, "Do you have any idea who this person might be?"

"No. I've had all the personnel files checked. No one stands out."

"And the students?"

Walking over to him, I glance at my father's collections. "They all come from the wealthiest families in America."

Hayden turns to me. "Even the wealthy can be unstable."

"True." I know most of the families. "I can't imagine it being one of the students."

"We'll find out soon enough," he murmurs.

With surprise, I look at him. "You think the person will try something with you here?"

"I know." Hayden crosses his arms. "I think this person has killed before. They're patient enough to not make a mistake. It takes more than one kill to learn that kind of patience." Bringing his eyes to mine, he continues, "You don't stop hunting, especially if you've wounded your prey. Us being here will only make him more determined to get to Jamie. She was his prey first, and he won't like sharing."

Fuck. It's hard to hear the facts.

"While we wait, Jamie should return to her normal routine. It will draw the perpetrator out into the open."

With everything Hayden just told me, it escalated my worry. I'll have to talk with Mason to take over some of my work for the time being, because I'll be spending every night with Jamie.

Chapter 24

Hello, beautiful.

Jamie

When I walk into the suite with Julian, Hayden, and Max, Kingsley stops chewing on a string of Twizzlers, and her mouth drops open. The piece of candy falls onto her lap as she stares wide-eyed at the two Navy Seals.

Swallowing hard, she then tilts her head. "You looked so badass coming in with an entourage."

"And here I was hoping no one would notice," I joke, knowing every student on campus probably knows I'm back and being guarded.

"Hayden and Max are family friends." I gesture to the couch. "Kingsley is one of my roommates and Mason's girlfriend."

They greet each other while I take a moment to drop my bag on my bed.

When I walk back into the living room, Julian takes hold of my hand, which has Kingsley's eyebrows popping up. "Oooh… I missed something good."

"Let's show Hayden and Max to their suite," Julian cuts in before I have to try and explain our relationship to Kingsley.

Before I shut the door behind us, I wink at Kingsley. "We'll talk before bed."

"We better!" she calls after me.

Walking toward the elevator, Hayden asks, "Can we take the stairs down."

"Sure."

We pause on the first step when Hayden checks the door and glances over the ceiling. "There's only the one camera?"

"There's one on every floor and in the hallways," Julian offers the information.

"None in the rooms, right?" Max asks.

"None. Privacy laws and all." Julian leads the way to the suite, which is opposite Preston's.

As Julian swipes the card, Preston's door opens, and he freezes the moment he sees us.

"Eve… evening, Sir… Sirs… Jamie," he stammers, his eyes wide on Hayden and Max.

"Preston," Julian greets with a nod, then glancing at Hayden, he explains, "Preston is my brother's assistant. He found the cameras."

"You did?" Max asks, taking a step closer to Preston.

When Preston's face pales, I walk to his side and hook an arm through his because I know how intimidating Max can be.

"I did… Sir."

Max lifts a finger to the jagged scar across his temple and rubs over it as if he's deep in thought. "How did you know to look for cameras?"

Preston swallows so hard I can hear it, then he adjusts his glasses. "I saw a YouTube video about hidden cameras, and since then, I always check."

"Smart." I feel Preston relax a little from the compliment.

"Let's head in, Max," Hayden says.

Yeah, I think Preston might pass out if we don't save him from Max soon.

I let the guys walk into the suite first, then give Preston's arm a hug. "You made a good impression on Max."

He shoves his hands in his pockets. "How do you know?"

I let out a burst of laughter. "Trust me, you'll know if he doesn't like you."

"Right." Preston begins to head toward the elevator while letting out a deep breath of air.

I walk into the suite and shut the door behind myself then go sit on the couch while Hayden and Max inspect their five-star lodgings.

"While you get settled, I'm going to take Jamie for a piano lesson," Julian says.

Hayden instantly frowns, which has me adding, "And we'll take the two guards downstairs along with us."

"Make sure they're always with you, and one always checks inside the building before you enter," Max rambles off orders.

"And when I have a class?" I ask for interest's sake.

Hayden smiles at me. "Then, Max and I will be sitting in the lecture hall with you."

"Oh, that's going to be so much fun for you," I joke. Getting serious again, I say, "Does that mean the guards have to be in the studio with us while I practice piano?"

Hayden immediately gets why I'm asking. "Have them stationed at the entrance and emergency exit." His eyes go to Julian. "Never leave her alone."

"Of course."

I get up and walk to the door with Max, mumbling, "Enjoy the date, lovebirds."

Julian

We wait with a guard outside the music building while the other checks inside.

With the all-clear, we head into the building, and the guards take their stations, one at the entrance and one at the back entrance, like Hayden instructed.

"Instead of a lesson, can you just play something?" Jamie asks as we sit down.

"Sure."

I begin to roll up the sleeves of my dress shirt when Jamie lets out a soft moan. "I love it when you do that."

"Yeah?" Lifting an eyebrow, I grin at her.

"Don't let it go to your head."

I place my hands on the keys, and ask, "Anything specific I should play?"

She doesn't even think before answering, "The piece you played in the restaurant."

A smile settles on my face when I begin to play. As my fingers glide to the right, my arm presses against Jamie's, and I feel the anticipation start to build.

Glancing at her, I watch as her eyes follow my hands until I play the last note.

Before I grab her and fuck her on the piano, I get up and walk over to the cello. "Would you like to hear something else?" My voice is low from the desire building inside me.

"Please," she whispers and turns on the piano bench to watch as I position the cello between my legs. "I might not hear a thing, though."

I let out a chuckle as I draw the bow across the strings. Midway into the piece, Jamie gets up from the chair and comes to kneel in front of me, her face showing every emotion I'm feeling.

Are we going to do this?

I see the answer in her eyes, *Yes.*

While the strings cry during a high note, I say, "There will be no turning back once we commit to a relationship."

Her eyes lock on mine. "I know."

Shifting forward on her knees, she takes the bow from my hand and sets it down on the floor. I move the cello to the side, and hardly have time to let it lean against the stand before Jamie moves closer. She places her hands on my thighs, and then her mouth is on mine.

Bringing my hands to her face, I cup her cheeks as my tongue slides inside her mouth. The kiss is slow and deep, then fast and filled with fire.

When Jamie slides her hands up my thighs, I break the kiss and press my forehead against hers. "Not here."

Her breaths burst against my lips, and it takes all my strength to not give in. Pulling back, I meet her eyes, dark with desire.

"My room?" she asks.

"Then the whole dorm will know what we're doing," I tease her to lighten the blow of rejection. Not that I'm rejecting her. "When we have sex again, I want to know I can take my time and enjoy you for an entire night without guards standing nearby."

My words bring a smile to her face, then she closes the distance between us. "So we can kiss?"

Letting out a chuckle, I press my mouth to hers.

Chapter 25

She's mine.

Jamie

Walking across campus, I feel every pair of eyes on me with Hayden and Max right behind me.

I try to block out the curious stares and think of the night before. Watching Julian play the cello reminded me of his hands on my body.

It's actually funny. Julian's one of the most powerful men I know, but he doesn't scare me. Not when there's a faceless man out there intent on killing me.

Maybe it's also because I got used to being around Carter and his friends.

"Is it true?" A random girl suddenly falls in next to me.

I glance over my shoulder at Hayden and Max before I frown at her. "What?"

"Is there a murderer on campus?" She glances around, looking at everyone with suspicion.

Not wanting to start a wildfire of rumors, I lie, "No, there's no murderer."

"Why do you have guards then?"

Before I can try to think of another lie, a group of girls block our way. "She's dating Julian Reyes."

Oh shit. I don't know which rumor would be worse for CRC.

"I'm not dating Julian," I quickly deny.

A girl with black hair steps a little forward, and lifting her chin, she says, "I saw the two of you together near the music center a couple of times."

I can't hide the irritation in my voice when I explain, "He's a friend of my family."

"No need to be defensive. We're just trying to get to know you better," the girl says, and when she tries to stand next to me and take hold of my arm, I pull away from her.

I can see where this is going. They think hanging out with me will give them a boost in status.

"I'm late for class." Pushing by them, the girls scatter to the side so Hayden and Max can pass.

"The two of you are going to have to hold me back, so I don't throat punch someone today," I mumble at them.

"Just keep your thumb on the outside of your fist," Max says, which has me chuckling.

I'm so annoyed by all the whispers and everyone staring at me. When I'm done attending all my classes, I decide to go for a jog before I start with an assignment.

I have a truckload of work to catch up on.

Hayden and Max left me with the two other guards, Joseph and Brian, and I can see they're not happy about jogging with me, but right now, I couldn't care less. I need the exercise, so I can unwind before my piano lesson tonight with Julian.

I can think of other ways to unwind, but...

I let out a frustrated sigh as I take the path into the woods to the left of the campus.

I don't feel as comfortable with Joseph and Brian as I do with Hayden and Max, so I only jog two miles before turning around and heading back in the direction of Trinity.

When I reach the suite, I go to my room and shower quickly before dressing in a pair of skinny jeans and a loose-fitting top that hangs off my left shoulder. Opting for boots, I forego my favorite pair of sneakers, and when I look at my reflection in the mirror, I grin.

I wonder if Julian's going to remember this outfit from the first night we met.

I walk out into the living room and sit on the sofa opposite Layla. She glances up from her laptop, then wiggles her eyebrows at me. "Someone looks good."

"Thank you."

A knock at the door has me jumping up. When I open it, my eyes go to Julian's face, and I watch for his reaction.

His gaze slowly moves down my body, and then the corner of his mouth lifts. "This outfit looks familiar."

"Yeah?"

He leans down and presses a kiss to my mouth before glancing over my head. "Hi, Layla."

"Hey, enjoy the lesson."

As we walk down the hallway, Julian takes hold of my hand and interlinks our fingers. Stepping into the elevator, I remember the incident from earlier. "People are starting to talk about us."

"Oh?" He lifts an eyebrow at me.

"Yeah, I told them you're a family friend, but if you hold my hand on campus, the lie's not going to stick."

"Why didn't you tell them the truth?"

We step out into the lobby, and the guards fall in behind us as we leave the dorm.

"I didn't know whether you were ready to go public."

Julian doesn't let go of my hand as we walk up the path to the music center, and it makes a warm feeling spread through my chest.

"Let's make it public," he murmurs as a group of students approach us.

"You sure? There's still time to back out," I tease, but I tighten my grip on his hand.

"I've never been surer."

The students give us a wide berth, but I notice how they look at our joined hands.

"Well, at least they'll have something new to talk about tomorrow," I say once they're out of earshot.

"What's the topic of gossip for today?" he asks while the guard goes into the building to check it.

"Whether there's a murderer loose on campus." A worried look flashes across Julian's features, which has me saying, "But that's old gossip. The way news spreads around here, I'm sure everyone knows by now that we were holding hands."

"I should probably give them something else to talk about." Julian lifts his other hand to the back of my neck and pulls me closer. His mouth presses softly against mine in a sweet kiss.

When he pulls back, I grin up at him, feeling happy about how things are progressing between us.

We finally get to go in, and this time, I sit down at the piano with the full intention of actually learning something tonight.

Julian takes a seat beside me, and when I begin to practice the keys he already taught me, his phone starts to ring.

"You can take the call," I say, my eyes not leaving the piano.

"I'll be right back." I hear him answer the phone as he walks out of the studio for some privacy.

I keep practicing, and every time I make a mistake, I mumble, "Shoot."

Minutes later, Julian comes back in, and sitting down again, he says, "You have to end with C and C."

"Which keys are those again?"

He places his hands on mine and starts from the beginning of the tune.

When we reach the end, I realize my mistake. "Ahh… that's why it sounded weird. Got it now."

I begin to practice again, trying to play faster, so it doesn't sound so choppy.

Julian's phone rings for a second time, which has me pausing to say, "You're a busy man tonight."

"Sorry," he apologizes as he gets up. "I'm busy with an international deal, and there's a time difference with the company being in Australia. I'll be right back."

"Don't worry." When he hesitates, I gesture for him to hurry along before his phone stops ringing. Julian walks out of the studio, leaving the door open behind him.

I keep practicing, and a smile grows on my face when it starts to sound better.

"Miss Truman?"

I glance up, and seeing one of the janitors standing in the doorway, I frown.

"There's a gas leak on campus. We've been asked to evacuate."

"Crap, are you serious?" I get up from the bench and walk toward him.

"Yes." He gestures toward the emergency exit at the back. "This way, please."

"What about Mr. Reyes?" I glance up the hallway and not seeing Julian, I begin to worry.

"He's already being escorted off-campus. We need to hurry."

He left without me?

Julian wouldn't leave me behind.

I stop before the emergency exit at the back of the building as a cold chill spreads over my body. My eyes dart to the janitor, and as I take a breath, he lunges for me. I don't have time to react as the back of my head is slammed against the wall, and a wave of darkness engulfs me

Chapter 26

That's right, walk away.

Julian

"We've included the exchange rate for today, but it will obviously be adjusted on the day we sign the contract," I say to the CEO of Lineage International. If we can close this deal, we'll have a foot in the import and export industry.

Standing right outside the main entrance, something sounds off, and it has me saying, "Please hold for a moment, Ms. Van Acker."

I pull the phone away from my ear and listen. When I don't hear Jamie playing the piano, I walk back inside the building.

Looking into the studio, I don't see her and glance up and down the hallway, as I call, "Jamie."

When she doesn't answer, I walk toward the back exit seeing as I was standing at the front the entire time I was on the call.

A glimpse of red on the wall up ahead catches my eye, and moving closer, I see blood. The sight sets off an explosion of emotions in my chest.

Cutting the call I'm on, I dial Hayden's number as I run the short distance to the back exit.

As I push through the door, Hayden answers his phone.

"He has Jamie!" Glancing around, I see Brian, lying unconscious outside the building. I quickly move to him and kneeling down, I check for his pulse. "Brian is down but alive. Jamie can't be far, though. I was only gone three minutes at the most."

"You left her alone?" I hear the anger in Hayden's voice, and it makes guilt weigh down on my shoulders.

I stood right by the front entrance of the music center.

How did I not hear anything?

Jamie would've put up a fight, she would've screamed.

"Get all the guards to help search for her," Hayden snaps just as I see him running up ahead.

I make the call to campus security while I run to catch up with him.

Noticing that we're heading toward the woods, I ask, "Do you really think he'd head this way with her?"

"Max is searching in the other direction in case he tries to leave the campus with her." Pointing a finger at me, he snaps, "You wait for the guards. Have them form a wide perimeter when they search. I'm going ahead."

I stop and watch as Hayden disappears into the trees, then glance back to see where the guards are.

Every inch of my skin feels like it's prickling. The realization of what happened begins to form around me like a dark cloud.

I left Jamie alone, and it only took three minutes for the bastard to grab her.

What the fuck have I done?

No deal was worth her safety. No amount of money can justify the fact that I left her unprotected.

I dart forward to search for her when Joseph calls out, "Mr. Reyes."

Noticing campus security right behind him, I don't stop running as I shout back, "Search for Jamie Truman!"

Running into the trees, I begin to shout her name over and over. "Jamie!"

My jacket gets snagged by a branch, and I quickly yank it off, dropping it on the ground as I keep moving.

"Jamie!"

Fear makes me push harder.

I have to find her.

Jamie

Coming to, the world spins while it feels like my head is going to explode.

I hear leaves crunching near my head, and the sound makes my pulse speed up until my blood is rushing through my veins. My mind clears a little as my thoughts begin to race.

The janitor.

Oh, God.

My eyes snap open, and with blurring vision, all I can make out is a hulking black mass looming over me, and it has panic and dread bleeding into my soul. I push up and try to move away, but the janitor lunges forward, and wrapping his hands around my neck, he slams the back of my head against the ground until stars explode behind my eyes.

I try to fight the dizzying haze enveloping me. Knowing I can't pass out, I fight the woozy feeling and blink faster so my eyes can adjust to the night.

I've never felt fear like this before. It paralyzes my body for a precious moment. With my vision fading, I fight to focus on the man in front of me, and in horror, I watch as he smiles down at me.

I've greeted this man.

I've seen him around campus multiple times.

My skin crawls at the realization, and my mind freezes in absolute terror as he tightens his grip around my neck. I gasp for breath as my eyes bore into his.

He looks different from what I thought he would.

He comes across as a normal man in his mid-thirties, and his smile almost looks loving.

I shake my head to rid myself of the shock that's prickling over my skin like tiny thorns. Everything begins to slow down around me until it's hard to focus on the reality. It's hard to make sense of what's happening. All I can hear is my thundering heart.

I manage to throw my body to the side, and it has him letting go of my neck. Feeling unsteady, I crawl backward to get away from him. I struggle to my feet even though my legs feel numb from the dread soaking into my skin.

He comes at me again, and I lunge to my right to avoid contact, but his hands wrap viciously around my neck, and he shoves me back down, slamming my head repeatedly against the ground. The brutal force steals my vision.

I hear a groan, but it sounds like it's miles away. Slipping in and out of consciousness as I fight not to pass out, his hands tighten their grip on my neck.

Fight, Jamie.

You have to fight.

Feeling out of it, I struggle to lift my arms but finally manage to grab hold of his hands.

I dig my feet into the ground and try to lift my body so I can throw him off of me again. His fingers slacken, and it gives me a moment's reprieve. Digging my nails into his skin, I scratch at him, but it only makes him tighten his hold on my neck again.

The sound of me gagging brings some clarity to my frazzled mind.

This man is going to kill me.

An isolated feeling wraps around me, making me cold as shivers rush over my body. My mind begins to race, searching for a way to free myself from this nightmarish moment.

"Jamie!" I hear Hayden's voice.

Hayden.

Hope floods through me, lending strength to my body.

"Hayden," I choke.

Digging my nails deeper into his skin, I yank against his hands and manage to scream, "Hayden!"

"Shut up! Shut up! Shut up!" the janitor begins to repeat over and over. He bashes my head against the ground again, causing a blinding pain to shudder through me.

"Jamie!"

Julian.

Hearing his horror-filled shout makes strength return to my body, and I yank harder against the janitor's hold.

"I'm here!" I scream as loud as I can.

They're here.

I'm going to be okay.

Fight, Jamie.

I keep yanking, and suddenly he lets go of me. I suck in desperate breaths as I watch him dart to my left as he runs deeper into the woods.

Feeling drained, I sob, "I'm here!" I struggle into the sitting position, my hand gently wrapping around my bruised neck.

Someone places a hand on my shoulder, making my head snap up.

"Which way did he go, Jamie?" Hayden asks.

It feels like I'm stuck in a trance as I glance up at Hayden, but I manage to point toward the left.

Someone drops down beside me, and when arms envelop me, I know it's Julian. The relief of having him with me makes my body sag into his.

All I hear is myself gasping for air as my heart pounds in my chest.

Chapter 27

Julian

Sitting next to the hospital bed, I can't tear my eyes away from Jamie. The nursing staff just brought her back from doing a CT scan.

Every couple of seconds, Jamie shivers while a nurse picks leaves and sticks out of her hair, placing them in a bag. Another nurse is tending to the gashes on the back of Jamie's head while a police officer hovers nearby to ensure the evidence is preserved.

I tighten my hold on her hand.

All it took was three minutes, and I almost lost her.

I'll never forgive myself.

I'm so fucking sorry.

Unable to say the words to her, I swallow the bitter taste of them down.

Throughout the entire time, the nursing staff is tending to her, Jamie doesn't say anything.

One of the nurses places a hospital gown at the foot of the bed, and says, "Miss Truman, we need to undress you, and then we'll put on the gown. Your clothes will go in this bag as evidence."

When Jamie doesn't move, I give her hand a squeeze, and ask, "Do you want me to stay?"

She barely moves as she nods.

Worried, I glance at the nurse.

"She's in shock. The sedative we gave her will help," she assures me, but it doesn't make me feel any better.

My eyes go to the police officer, and I ask, "Can we have some privacy?" I can see he's going to argue, and it makes me glare at him. "You can wait right outside the room, but I insist on privacy while my girlfriend changes."

Reluctantly, he says, "I want to talk to Miss Truman as soon as she's changed into the hospital gown."

I wait for the man to leave before I get up and bending over Jamie, I help her to stand. Once I'm sure she's not going to fall down, I step to the side so the nurse can undress Jamie.

Before the nurse helps Jamie into the hospital gown, I quickly scan over her body, needing to know she's not hurt anywhere else.

The moment the nurse steps away to open the door for the officer, I take hold of Jamie and help her back on the bed.

I steal a moment to press a kiss to her forehead and closing my eyes, I whisper, "I'm so fucking sorry I left you alone."

The words sound… futile.

Sometimes it's just too late to apologize. The damage has been done, leaving me with the devastating consequences of my actions.

"You can come back in," I hear the nurse say, which has me taking hold of her hand with both of mine to lend her strength while the officer questions her.

"Miss Truman, I need to ask you questions. Every little detail is important. Can you tell me in your own words what happened?"

Jamie swallows a couple of times, then murmurs in a toneless voice, "The janitor…"

"Henry Little?" Glancing at me, the officer confirms, "Little is employed as a janitor at Trinity Academy?"

"Yes, I've already handed his personnel file over to another officer."

Nodding, he turns his attention back to Jamie. "You were saying, Miss Truman."

"The janitor… Henry Little…" Jamie seems to drift off for a moment before she continues with a hoarse but stronger voice, "He told me there was a gas leak. We had to evacuate. He banged my head against the wall."

"Can we go back to before Henry Little approached you. What were you busy doing?"

"I was busy with a piano lesson."

The questioning continues, and it guts me to hear her repeat her answers over and over again, but I know it needs to be done to help the police catch the bastard.

After the officer finished with the questioning, a nurse moved Jamie to a private room.

Rhett and Miss Sebastian come into the room, and Miss Sebastian immediately goes to hug Jamie.

Framing Jamie's face, Miss Sebastian begins to ask, "What's your name?"

Jamie frowns, and slurs as she answers, "Jamie Truman."

Miss Sebastian gives her a tearful smile. "How old are you?"

Jamie blinks a couple of times before murmuring, "Nineteen."

"Where were you born?"

It takes a couple of seconds before Jamie responds, "Saluda."

Miss Sebastian lets out a breath of relief, then hugs Jamie again once she's seemingly satisfied with evaluating Jamie's memory and concentration skills.

Rhett comes to stand in front of me, and I see the same anger on his face that's burning inside of me.

"Carter will be here any minute. What did the doctor say?"

"They did a CT scan. There's no serious brain injury. They said they would check on her routinely because of the concussion she sustained."

Rhett glances at Jamie, and there's a flash of pain on his face seeing the state she's in. "What did they say about her neck?"

"There's severe bruising, but no permanent damage has been done to her airway and vocal cords. She'll be hoarse for a couple of days while it heals."

Rhett nods, then locking eyes with me he asks, "How did the fucker get his hands on her?"

Just as I'm about to answer, Mason comes into the room with Carter, having picked him up from the airport.

Seeing the rage on Carter's face, I square my shoulders and expecting the blow, I keep still as his fist connects with my jaw. The man packs quite the punch, and I move my jaw to ease the ache.

"You fucking left her alone?" he shouts.

"Carter." Jamie tries to sit up and not wanting her moving, I quickly place a hand on her arm.

"It's okay. Lie back."

Carter takes a couple of deep breaths to reign in his temper, and it gives Jamie time to say, "Don't blame Julian." She swallows hard before continuing, "I shouldn't have left the studio."

Carter shakes his head hard and pushing past me, he leans over Jamie and engulfs her in his arms. "Don't blame yourself."

"I was so stupid," she whimpers, her voice hardly recognizable.

"None of this is your fault," Carter reassures her.

He's right because the blame rests squarely on my shoulders.

Chapter 28

Jamie

The past couple of days have been crazy, to say the least. My friends and family are trying to be strong for me, but I can see they're buckling under the weight of the frustration and worry. It's not just my life that's been disrupted by this nightmarish hell.

Carter almost lost his mind, and it took a lot to get him to ease up. I'm worried what this will do to Della's health with her being so close to her delivery date.

I let out a deep sigh.

So many worries. So much trauma.

How do I even begin to deal with it all?

A psychiatrist came to see me, but I declined his offer for counseling. I have a supportive family, and I'll talk to Julian if I need to.

Sitting in the car as Julian drives us to The Rose Acre, I stare at nothing in particular.

Henry Little.

Such an ordinary name. An unassuming face.

I doubt my judge of character because never in a million years would I have suspected the janitor who always smiled, could be capable of such inhumaneness.

When Julian brings the car to a stop in front of the entrance, I climb out and glance at the vehicle stopping behind us and see Hayden and Max get out. While Hayden scans our surroundings, Max immediately walks to my side and placing his hand on my back, he murmurs, "I'm always two steps behind you. Let's go inside."

Glancing at Julian, I see the guilt eating away at him. Reaching for his hand, I intertwine our fingers, then we walk inside the luxurious hotel.

I'll be staying with Julian until I've made a full recovery. After that, I have no idea what I'll do.

Walking into the suite, Hayden and Max first check every room.

"I had the hotel swap the bed in the other room for two queens," Julian says.

Glancing around the penthouse suite, I'm relieved to see it's big, so at least there's enough space for the four of us while we're here. The first time I was here, I didn't pay much attention to my surroundings, and now all the luxury means nothing.

My world has been dulled, the beauty stolen from it.

Julian takes my bag to his room and giving Hayden and Max a small smile, I follow after him.

I close the bedroom door behind us and wait for Julian to place my bag next to the bed. He first looks at me before he closes the distance between us. He begins to reach for the back of my neck, but then he stops and draws back.

"Sorry, it's become a habit."

Taking hold of his hand, I bring it up to my face and press my cheek to his palm.

My body shudders at the familiar touch, and it has Julian stepping closer. He wraps his other arm around me and slowly moves his hand to my jaw. His worried eyes scan over my face.

Feeling drained from all the emotional strain and trauma, I take a shaky breath while I fight back the tears for the hundredth time.

"I'm so sorry, Jamie," he whispers, his face tightening with regret and sorrow over what has happened to me.

I bring my hands up between us and take hold of his jacket's lapels. "It's not your fault. Stop blaming yourself."

He shakes his head and presses his forehead against mine. "I almost lost you. It fucking terrifies me."

"I'm still here," I try to comfort him. "I'm stronger than I look."

Closing the remaining distance between us until our bodies touch, Julian presses a kiss to every bruise on my face, then his mouth moves to my neck. He's so gentle with me, it makes it so much harder not to cry.

Bringing his eyes back to mine, he must see I'm struggling because he wraps his arms tightly around me and whispers, "Cry, Jamie. No one will see."

As if my tear ducts were waiting to hear those words, I'm unable to stop myself. I tighten my hold on his jacket and press my forehead to his shoulder, trying to smother the first sob.

"I'm here," he whispers close to my ear.

Nodding, I press closer to him.

Julian's grip on me releases, but it's only for a moment so he can slip his arms under me. Lifting me to his chest, he walks us over to the armchair. He sits down and positions me sideways on his lap, so my legs can rest over the side of the chair.

Cradling me, he keeps whispering words of comfort until I drift off from exhaustion.

Waking with a start, my breaths rush over my lips.

Arms tighten around me, and I hear Julian whisper, "It's okay. I'm here."

He's still sitting with me on his lap, and it makes my body relax against his.

"Aren't you tired?" I ask.

"No. I'll sit with you for as long as it takes," he murmurs.

I pull back and force a smile to my lips. "You can't be comfortable in a suit." I begin to shift off his lap, but he drops a hand to my hip to stop me. Glancing at him, I say, "At least change out of the suit. I'll sleep on the bed."

Julian pushes his arms under me and getting up, he carries me over to the bed where he gently places me down.

My eyes follow him as he walks to a dresser. He pulls a pair of sweatpants out and then drops them on the bed.

He unbuttons his suit jacket and shrugging it off, he first goes to hang it up before he steps out of his shoes.

The moment feels intimate while I watch him undress. There's no sexual tension as I take in the gorgeous sight of him. I've never spent this much time with a man before.

Julian has been by my side ever since this mess started. We haven't had a chance to enjoy each other like other couples do, and it makes me worry whether our newborn romance will survive this nightmare.

After pulling on the sweatpants, he lies down on the bed and gently lifts my head so he can push his arm under it. I snuggle closer to him until our bodies are pressed together, and rest my head on his shoulder.

Julian presses his mouth to the top of my head and takes a deep breath, then asks, "How do you feel?"

"I'm okay," I answer automatically, hesitant to share my worries about us with him.

The look of concern never eases from his face. "And your head? You'll tell me if it hurts?"

Lifting my face to his, I press a soft kiss to his mouth. "You're so caring."

His arms wrap around me, and he holds me as if he's scared I'll vanish into thin air if he relaxes for a second.

My new worry wins out, and I ask, "Do you think our relationship will survive this mess?"

I have never been a needy person, and the feeling is a foreign one.

I hate it.

This attack has stripped me of my self-confidence.

Julian brings his hand to my jaw and gently nudges it up, so I'll look at him. "What made you ask that question?"

I swallow hard before I answer, "It's a lot of pressure getting involved with someone who…" my words trail away as I'm unable to finish the sentence.

He leans in and presses a kiss to my mouth. "There's no pressure, Jamie. Yes, I'm worried and fear for your safety, but that doesn't affect how I feel about you."

How do you feel about me?

As if he can read my thoughts, he says, "I'm not going to tell you I love you. Not now. You wouldn't believe the words, and in all honesty, you deserve more than a confession that's overshadowed by trauma."

Although I understand his reasoning, it doesn't lessen my worry.

"Hey, look at me."

My eyes drift back to his.

"I'm committed to you, Jamie. Through the good and the bad. Once this is over, we'll get to enjoy each other."

When this is over.

"Will it ever end?" My voice sounds hollow because there's no hope left in me.

"The police now know who he is. They'll find him," Julian assures me.

"Why me?" I ask, even though none of us have an answer.

Julian tightens his hold on me and presses soft kisses to my forehead, my cheeks, and my jaw.

Clinging to each other, I try not to think of the cold treat of death creeping closer.

But there's a reason I'm still standing.

Focusing on Julian's face and seeing how much he cares about me only makes me more determined to survive this killer.

I have to fight for Della.

I have to fight for everyone I love.

I'm going to fight for myself.

Chapter 29

Julian

I've been working from home for the past three days. Lake came over today with all the work Jamie has missed out on, and I'm relieved to see that it's helping to distract her.

Lake opens his laptop, then says to Jamie, "This is the paper I did on international law. Read through it while I order us some snacks."

Getting up, he grins at me. "I'm putting it all on your tab."

I let out a chuckle. "I'm totally okay with that."

After Lake has placed an order for an obscene amount of food, we move to the balcony so we won't bother Jamie.

"With everything going on, we haven't spent much time together," I say as I stare out over the city.

"Yeah." He leans against the banister. "I thought you'd want to know that I've spoken with my father. He's willing to stay on for another four years. He said he'd talk to you once you're back at the office."

I've totally forgotten about the problem of Mr. Cutler retiring.

Placing my hand on Lake's shoulder, I say, "Thank you." My eyes drift back to Jamie. "Thank you for helping her." In the spur of the moment, I pull him into a hug. "I owe you so much."

"Don't worry about it. We're family," Lake murmurs.

"I hate to break up your bromance," Jamie's voice pulls us apart, "but I need Lake to explain this sentence to me because it feels like I'm reading a foreign language."

Lake lets out a chuckle as he hurries over to her. "Which one?"

Minutes after the food arrives, I receive a call from reception that Detectives Olsen and O'Neal are here.

While waiting for the two men to come up, Jamie begins to chew on her thumbnail. I take hold of her hand and weave our fingers together.

Hayden opens the door for the two Detectives, and when we're all seated, Detective Olsen says, "We've looked into Henry Little's family history and prior places of employment." The detective clears his throat. "He comes from a middle-class family. Previous employers all say he was a good worker, and they never had any problems with him."

"In other words, you found nothing that will be helpful?" Hayden asks.

"Actually, we did find something," Detective O'Neal takes over. "After searching through his home, we found items that could be mementos he kept from potential previous victims. We're looking into unsolved cases to see if we can link any to Henry Little."

"So, he has killed before?" Jamie asks, her face going ghost white.

"We're still looking into it, Ma'am." Shifting in his chair, Detective O'Neal says, "We'd just like to go over some of the details you gave in your statement."

They only spend another ten minutes with Jamie before they leave, promising to let us know if they learn anything new.

The moment Hayden closes the door behind them, he says, "They're not telling us everything."

Lake, who's been quiet the entire time, suddenly asks, "Should I ask Preston to hack into their system for the file."

"He can do that?" Max asks.

Lake nods, already pulling his phone from his pocket.

Hayden is deep in thought as he murmurs, "The more information we have on Henry Little, the better."

While Lake is on the phone with Preston, Jamie gives me a tired smile. "I'm going to take a nap."

"Let's just hear what Lake says, then I'll go with you," I say, not wanting her out of my sight.

Lake hangs up, then grins. "He'll get right on it. I'm going to head home. I'll call you as soon as Preston has anything."

"Thanks for all your help today," I say as I walk him to the door.

Jamie gives him a hug. "I really appreciate you bringing my assignments over."

"Just let me know if you need help with any of them. I'm only a call away."

"Will do."

I shut the door behind Lake, then taking Jamie's hand, I pull her toward the bedroom.

"I guess we'll watch baseball," I hear Max mutter before I close the door behind us.

"You don't have to stay with me every second of the day," Jamie says as soon as we're alone. "You must have a lot of work to do."

"I can answer emails from my phone."

She lets out a sigh then goes to use the ensuite restroom. My eyes never leave the door while she's in there, and I feel the familiar panic clawing up my spine from her being out of my sight.

The moment she walks back into the room, I let out a deep breath.

I wait for her to crawl onto the bed before I sit down next to her. She first snuggles against my side before I pull my phone out.

Even though I open my email account, I can't focus on any of the words. Giving up, I set the device down on the bedside table, and look down at Jamie's face.

Lifting my hand to her head, I softly pull my fingers through her hair, careful to avoid the area where her stitches are healing.

I have no words to describe what I felt when we found her, and I saw her all bloody and gasping for air on the ground.

I thought the night I got the call that Jennifer had died was the worst night of my life, but I was wrong.

I continue to softly caress Jamie's hair and try to think back to when things changed between us but can't. It feels like I've always cared about her. I now also understand what Mason must've gone through with Kingsley.

Almost losing Jamie to such a senseless violent act, I realized one thing. If the worst had happened, I would've died out in those woods with her.

Chapter 30

No matter where you go, you're mine.

Jamie

Since Julian went back to the office two days ago, I've been spending all my time catching up on the work I've missed. A couple of times, I had to call Lake for help, and I feel lucky that I have him to lean on, or I'd have to drop this semester.

Hayden and Max have been working in Julian's study on the file Preston managed to get for them.

Glancing around the living room while I stretch my neck, which is healing nicely, I wonder whether I'll be able to go back to Trinity Academy after almost being killed there.

Julian hasn't told me anything about what the reaction is at the academy or with the press, but I'm sure news has gotten out by now.

Just added pressure for Julian to deal with.

My phone begins to buzz next to me, and I smile when I see Julian's name flashing on the screen. He's been so protective of me, which is only making me fall harder for him.

"Hey," I answer. "Missing me already?"

"Yeah, I wanted to check on you before I go into a meeting. What are you doing?" he asks.

"I just finished a paper." I lean back against the couch, feeling relaxed now that I get to hear his voice again, even though I just saw him five hours ago.

"Would you like to go out for dinner tonight?"

A smile spreads over my face at the thought of getting out for a while. "I'd like that."

"Great. I'll make reservations for seven."

"I'll miss you until then," I whisper, feeling the warmth from falling in love with Julian spread through my body.

"Miss you too," he replies.

I cut the call and open my laptop, so I can start with the next paper.

I'm researching a topic when my phone vibrates again. Not recognizing the number, I let it go to voicemail.

Just as I get back into reading an article, my phone beeps. Frowning, I pick it up and first finish reading the paragraph before I unlock my phone. Seeing that it's a message, I click on it and then stare at a photo of Julian. He's wearing the same grey suit from this morning and standing at a desk while reading a document.

Confused, I look at the number that sent me the photo.

Strange, I don't recognize the sender.

My phone begins to ring again and seeing it's the same number that sent me the photo, I answer, "Hello?"

"Hello." There's a moment's pause. "I've missed you. Have you missed me?"

"Excuse me?" I frown and pulling the phone away from my ear, I look at the number again before I ask, "Who's this?"

"Ahh… you're hurting my feelings, little girl."

Realization dawns on me, and it blazes through me like a wildfire.

No.

I move to get up so I can call Hayden and Max, but then he says, "If you tell anyone, your boyfriend dies."

I instantly freeze, my body tense as I wait to hear what he wants.

"Come to CRC Holdings."

"And then?" I ask as my heart begins to beat faster.

"Then, we can spend some time together." His voice sounds so normal, it's hard to process that I'm talking to a killer. "Come to me, and I won't kill your boyfriend. If you call the police, he dies. If you bring anyone along with you, he dies. Tick tock, little girl. His time is running out."

The line cuts out, and instantly my phone beeps again with another photo of Julian talking to a woman.

Fear bubbles up in my chest, making it feel like I'm being suffocated.

Photos pop up on my phone, one after the other.

Knowing I have to hurry, I grab a piece of paper and write a note for Hayden and Max.

Henry Little threatened Julian's life. I've gone to CRC Holdings. Please come.

Checking my watch, I add the time, and then I dart out of the front door while Hayden and Max are still busy in the study.

Rushing out of the hotel, I hail a cab and give the driver CRC's address. I know Hayden and Max will be right behind me because they will check on me soon, and seeing I'm gone, they'll find the note.

They have to.

My heart's beating out of my chest as the cab takes me closer to CRC.

There are guards there. I'll cause a scene, and Henry will be arrested.

For a moment, I close my eyes, my skin coming alive with pins and needles.

Today this madness ends, and I take back my life.

As we near CRC, my eyes dart around the area for any sign of the janitor.

I ask the cab to stop across the road from the office, and after settling the fee, I climb out. I keep glancing around me, feeling a sense of reasonable safety because I'm surrounded by people.

There are empty vehicles lining the street, and there's an officer standing on the corner, busy issuing a ticket to a delivery van.

My phone beeps, and I quickly pull it out of my pocket.

Come inside, little girl.

Shoving the device back into my pocket, my eyes dart to the building. The windows are all darkened, and I can't see inside.

Slowly, I begin to cross the street. My eyes dart to the officer, and I feel a sense of panic as he walks further down the block.

Crap.

Taking a deep breath to calm my frail nerves, I turn my eyes back to the building in front of me.

I've just stepped onto the sidewalk when someone bumps into me. Something presses against my arm, and it instantly feels like a swarm of bees is trying to crawl through my skin.

Fear drags me under as I begin to lose control of my body, and I'm shoved inside a van.

Chapter 31

Julian

My phone begins to ring, and I pause as I glance at the screen. Seeing Hayden's name, I push my chair back. "Excuse me. There's an emergency."

I walk out of the boardroom as I answer my phone, "What's wrong?"

"Jamie left the suite. Is she with you?"

"No, I'm in a meeting. What's going on?"

"Little made contact with her and threatened to kill you, so she snuck out without telling us first. We're pulling up to CRC."

"What?"

My breaths slow down as the world warps around me.

"Julian? Are you listening?"

This is not happening.

Not again.

"I'm on my way down. Meet me out front."

The shock begins to lift, and adrenaline begins to pulse through my body. Darting forward, I run for the elevator and slam the button a couple of times before the doors slide open.

Horror fills every corner of my soul, and it feels like the walls are closing in on me. I begin to breathe faster, and as the doors open, I run out of the elevator into the lobby. Seeing Hayden and Max outside the entrance looking around for Jamie, I head toward them.

Hayden spots me first, and as I reach him, I ask, "Any sign of her?"

The worried look on Hayden's face is answer enough for me.

Desperately, I glance around, and when there's no sign of her, I say, "Preston can trace Jamie's phone. We need to leave now."

Max takes hold of my arm as he begins to walk away from the building with Hayden right behind us. "Call Preston and get him to do the trace. Don't try to phone Jamie. You'll only give away the fact that she has her phone on her, if he doesn't already know, and we'll lose the only way to find her."

I yank out my phone and make the call as I climb into the back of Hayden's SUV, putting the call on speakerphone so Hayden and Max can hear.

"Preston Culpepper speaking."

"It's Julian. Can you trace Jamie's phone and tell us where she is."

"Yes, Sir." I hear him shuffle something around. "What's her number?"

I ramble it off as Hayden steers the SUV in the direction the van sped off in.

A minute later, Preston says, "The signal is heading northwest on CA 150 W toward Black Mountain Fire Rd."

Thank God, her phone is still working and with her.

"Send me the location and keep me updated every minute," I order.

The moment the call cuts, Max says, "Hand me the bag from the back."

It's heavy when I pick it up, but I pass it to the front between the two seats. "Hayden says you know how to fire a gun."

It doesn't sound like a question, but I answer anyway, "Yes."

"Good. Just point this thing away from Hayden and me, and we'll be good." He hands me a colt, and the metal feels heavy and foreign in my hand.

Staring down at the weapon, there's no doubt in my mind that I'll kill Henry Little first chance I get.

My phone beeps with the new location, and I quickly update Hayden.

"The road leads past Trinity Academy. It's mountain terrain," Max says, having pulled up a map on his phone.

Placing the gun next to me on the seat, I shrug out of my jacket and roll up the sleeves of my dress shirt. Removing my tie, I toss it to the side and unbutton the top two buttons, hoping to breathe easier, but it doesn't help.

Taking hold of the gun again, I close my eyes and pray we're not too late.

Chapter 32

Jamie

"It's time, little girl. It's time."

The words pour hot lava through my veins. For what feels like the hundredth time, I glance around the empty van, but I'm only surrounded by the white panels.

"There we go," Henry says, his voice calm as he climbs into the back.

I turn my head, and the moment I lay eyes on him, my heartbeat speeds up, and my mind repels at being face to face with a killer.

I'm too scared to move, but I know I have to do something. My right hand is cuffed to the gate, separating the cab from the back of the van.

It happened so fast. Henry tazed, and cuffed me within seconds.

I push my body closer to the gate and away from him, keeping my eyes trained on Henry.

"Finally, we get to be alone."

The shock of what's happening is still vibrating through me, numbing my emotions.

Henry casually moves closer to me, and I instantly react by kicking at him.

"Now, now, I'm not going to kill you yet. I just want your phone," he tsks.

Keep calm.

Think.

Okay, don't antagonize him.

He moves slowly again, holding one hand up in the air while pulling my phone from my pocket with the other.

"There, that wasn't so hard, was it?"

I watch as he takes my phone apart, crushing the sim card under his heel. "Don't want any visitors, now do we?"

A song plays softly from the cab, and it only increases the eeriness of being at the mercy of this man who seems utterly normal.

"Why did you listen to me?" he asks. "Why did you come to me? Now you're never going to get away."

Holy shit.

"I have people looking for me." Why I chose to say that of all things and not demand that he lets me go, I don't know.

It's because I know Julian, Hayden, and Max won't stop looking. They found me before. They will find me again. I have to believe that.

Ignoring my words, his smile widens for a moment. "You shouldn't have come." Letting out a sigh, he continues, "Why did you do such a stupid thing? You shouldn't have come."

I frown at the words, realizing he's placing the blame on me.

Is he trying to ease his conscience?

Does he even have one?

"Why me?" I ask, needing to know why he's intent on taking my life.

"You smiled at me," he chuckles. There's a caring look on his face as if we're old friends. "You have a pretty face, and you smiled. How was I supposed to not react?"

My eyes lock on his, and I expected them to be vacant, or at least, to show some sign of insanity, but they are brown and just… normal.

When he moves again, I cower back against the gate, but instead of lunging at me, he makes himself comfortable, leaning back against the side panel. He folds his hands together on his lap and tilting his head, he again smiles at me.

"It wasn't supposed to happen this way."

Clearing my throat, I hate that my voice is trembling as I ask, "What?"

"It was supposed to look like suicide, but your friends just couldn't leave well enough alone."

Is he referring to the night he cut my wrist?

I clear my throat and lifting my eyes from his hands, I bring them to his face. "Henry..."

"Mhhh... say my name again," he interrupts me.

Uhm... okay?

"H-Henry," I stammer as dread causes my throat to close. My breaths speed up until my mouth is bone dry. "What are you going to do to me?"

He takes a deep breath and first lets it out. Glancing at the panel opposite him, he thinks for a moment.

That's a good sign, right? Maybe he hasn't planned this through, and I have a chance of convincing him to let me go?

Before I can open my mouth to reason with him, he begins to talk, "The first time it happened... ah... I was twenty-three. Pretty, but not particularly pretty. Brown hair." He tilts his head, his expression as if the memory is a fond one as he glances at my hair. "Passed out on the floor of the living room. It just happened that the girl was there when I felt it coming on. I closed the damper to the fireplace."

Wanting to keep him talking so I can buy myself more time, I ask, "Henry, what do you mean by you felt it coming on?"

Pulling up one leg, he positions himself into a more comfortable pose. He lowers his head and glances sideways at me, resting his forearm on his knee.

"Well, it's hard to describe..." he clears his throat, "...to put into words. It's not like I blacked out..." Swallowing, he glances at me, "...or felt like I was possessed." He clears his throat again, his mouth slightly arching higher. "I remember every moment in detail." He lifts his other hand to his face and rubs his pointer finger over his left eyebrow. "What they looked like, what they wore, how they smelled." Lifting his head, his eyes lock on me for a fraction of a second. "I get to keep them forever that way. Just like we'll always be together."

Everything about him is so casual, it's unnerving. It feels like he's trying to distract me with his movements.

"Them? How many victims have there been, Henry?"

He looks annoyed for a moment. "A couple... fifteen... no, seventeen."

The breath stalls in my throat.

He's murdered so many people, and knowing this, kills the tiny seed of hope I've been nurturing in my chest.

He must see the horror on my face because his smile falters. "I mean, the thing is…" He seems to recover as the tension eases from his features, leaving him looking charismatic again, "what is your passion? You know? If you get to do the one thing you love most in this world." His gaze lingers on me for longer this time. "You're so present in the moment…" he lightly shakes his head, a chuckle escaping, "it's as if… you're in control of everything."

My breaths become short puffs, each one laced with dread, and I feel my defenses rearing to life. "How would you feel if someone killed one of your loved ones?"

"Oh…" he smirks, "I certainly wouldn't appreciate it."

"But…but," I stammer, "You murder innocent people. You take them from their families. How can you do that to another person?"

"Oh… I have an answer for that." He sits up straighter, excitement flashing across his face. "It's been smacked up inside my head a time or two. You know? I've thought hard about that." His tongue darts out to wet his lips. "But there's this sensation of watching the life drain away from someone. You can almost taste the air changing."

Absolutely horrified and repelled by what he's saying, I ask, "Don't you regret it? Don't you feel some sort of... remorse for what you have done?"

"Well, the first time..." he tilts his head, thinking. "I can still see it in slow motion." His lips curve up. "The morning after I was shocked," he nods as he looks directly into my eyes, "I felt awful," dropping his eyes, he wets his lips again, "but after that, it became more routine. You know? The rush faded."

I never take my eyes away from him, and with every word leaving his mouth, with every gesture – it makes it clear this man has no feelings.

He's mimicking the expression and actions he knows will put me at ease.

Realizing that all the talking in the world isn't going to stop him from killing me, it makes shivers race over my body as I begin to tremble uncontrollably.

He's so observant of my reactions and feelings that his facial expression changes to being guarded, as I'm overcome with angst and desperation.

"Well..." he clears his throat and shifts his body into a crouching position. Giving me a tender smile, he continues, "I suppose it's time."

I push myself back against the gate, and it makes him slowly inch closer. The moment he's close enough, I begin to kick out at him, and it has him holding up his hands. "Don't panic. It will be quick."

He lunges at me, and it tears a desperate scream from me. His body towers over mine, and I see a flash of pain on his face as I manage to knee him where it hurts most.

Anger darkens his face until it shows the real monster hiding behind the façade.

"You could've gone peacefully like the others."

He uses more strength, which is by far greater than my own, and wraps his hands around my neck. Trying to defend myself, the cuffs cut into my right wrist when I yank on them.

"Just go peacefully."

"No!" The word sounds garbled, and I first try to pry his hands away with mine, but when that doesn't help ease his grip on my neck, I begin to hit and scratch his face. During our struggle, I manage to claw at his right eye, and it has him drawing back.

He first presses a hand to his face and checks for blood, then hisses, "Now look what you've done."

He raises his arm, and I take the chance to kick him in the gut. The windshield up front suddenly explodes, and I watch as Henry falls back. He writhes for a second then pulling himself into a crawling position, he struggles to the rear of the van, and away from me.

My mind races to catch up with what's happening, leaving me feeling drained and dizzy.

My breaths continue to race over my dry lips as an intense distraught feeling swamps me.

Chapter 33

Julian

My heart is beating out of my chest as I stalk closer to the rear of the van while Hayden moves to the front. I hear glass shatter and realize Max must've taken a shot. Yanking the door open, I zero in on Little, where he's crawling toward me.

Scanning over him, and seeing that he's unarmed, I reach inside and grabbing hold of his collar, I drag him out of the van. He stumbles, and before he can regain his balance, I shove him down to the ground.

"Don't fucking move," I shout as I keep the gun trained on him. I dare a glance inside the van and check for Jamie. "Are you okay, Jamie?" I call out, turning my gaze back to Little.

"Yes."

Hayden comes up behind Little and keeping his gun pointed at the scum, he checks inside the van as well, then he looks at me.

My hand begins to shake from all the strain it's taking to not just shoot the bastard as rage burns inside of me.

The only way to stop this monster is by killing him.

Hayden first signals to Max, who took up a position five hundred yards away to come down, then looks at me. "I'll uncuff Jamie."

Climbing in the back of the van, Hayden pulls the door shut behind him, and I appreciate that Jamie won't see this. She's been traumatized enough by this fucker.

"You can't kill me," Little says smugly as he keeps a hand over the flesh wound Max gave him in his arm while he rises to his feet.

He terrorized the woman I love.

He strangled her.

The thoughts make my finger tighten on the trigger.

He makes eye contact with me for a fraction of a second, and the smile drops from his face.

"Go to hell, Little," I murmur as I pull the trigger.

His body slumps backward, and blood trickles down his face. Pointing the gun at his chest, I pull the trigger twice to ensure he's dead.

Max reaches me, and I immediately hand the gun to him. I stare at the body of the man who made Jamie's life a living hell before I open the door. My eyes land on Jamie, where she's cowering against Hayden.

"Is it done?" Hayden asks.

"Yeah, all clear," Max calls over my shoulder.

Jamie moves forward, and I reach for her, wrapping my arms around her as I pull her out of the vehicle and turning her away from the body.

I move us around the side of the van before I sink to the ground, cradling her against me.

The relief of holding her and knowing the nightmare is finally over is so overwhelming it pushes emotion up my throat. I begin to check her for any injuries, and ask, "Are you okay? Did he hurt you?"

"I'm okay," she whispers, her grip on me as tight as she can manage.

Her body shivers violently, and it makes me hold her tighter.

"Oh, God. I'm so glad you're okay," I whisper as my own emotions come crashing down around me.

Jamie lifts a hand to cover her mouth and then lurching away from me, she bends forward, and her body begins to jerk. I quickly gather her hair in one hand then use my other to rub her back as she heaves.

"Let's get rid of the body," I hear Hayden say under his breath. "You're out of practice. How could you only clip his arm?"

"I didn't aim to kill," Max grumbles. "Grab the head."

Jamie sits back on the ground, her face pale, which has me saying, "Just a couple of minutes, and we'll get you out of here."

She nods, then lifts her eyes to mine. "He was so normal," she whispers, still caught in a bubble of trauma.

"Did he do anything to you?" I ask to make sure she's not hurt.

Jamie shakes her head and looking bewildered, she says, "We mostly talked."

Hayden and Max come back, and while they're wiping the van clean of all evidence, I pick up Jamie and carry her back to where the SUV is parked.

Only Hayden climbs in the car, and says, "I'm taking you back to the hotel while Max takes care of the evidence. Make sure Preston doesn't talk."

"He won't," I assure him.

"It's over?" Jamie whispers. She lifts her eyes to me, searching my face for the answer.

"It's over." I press a kiss to her forehead, holding her close to my chest.

Chapter 34

Jamie

The second we get home, I go to the bathroom, needing to wash the nightmare off of me.

If that's at all possible.

I'm busy taking a shower when the full impact of what happened shudders through me again. My movements slow down as I rinse the suds from my body until my arms fall limply to my sides.

I keep hearing his words.

'There's this sensation of watching the life drain away from someone. You can almost taste the air changing.'

'Don't panic. It will be quick.'

'Just go peacefully.'

The words gnaw at my frail nerves, and I sink down to the tiled floor.

"Jamie, are you okay in there?" Julian calls from the other side of the door.

"I'm not sure," I murmur, my mind still stuck in the back of the van.

I hear the door open, and then Julian turns off the water before he crouches next to me. My head feels heavy as I tilt it back to look at him.

"I'm not sure what to feel," I admit.

"That's totally understandable," he says as he slips his hands under me. Lifting me out of the shower, he takes me over to the counter and sets me down. He first dries me, then wraps me in a bathrobe before carrying me to the bed.

After he sets me down, he strips out of his damp dress shirt and suit pants, then slides in next to me.

"We seem to be meeting here a lot," I say. Reaching for his hand, I bring it closer and press a kiss to his skin. "Thank you."

Thank you for killing him.

"It had to be done," he murmurs. "You understand, right?"

Not wanting him feeling any guilt or remorse for what he's done to protect me, I nod. "I do. The world will be a better place without him in it."

Julian glances over my face, then he asks, "How's your head? He didn't hurt you again?"

I shake my head and snuggle closer to him. "He tried to strangle me, but it was briefly. This time I could fight back, and y'all were there pretty quickly."

There's a moment's silence, then Julian asks, "You said you talked with him?"

I nod, and wrapping an arm around Julian's waist, I rest my cheek over his heart.

"He didn't come across as some crazy creep. The way he spoke and his gestures – he almost seemed charismatic... friendly." I pause for a moment before I admit, "I think that scared me more than if he had been insane and railed at me."

"I'm sorry this happened," Julian says. "Why didn't you tell Hayden or Max? Why did you go to CRC?"

I shift back and move my head to a pillow, so I can see Julian. "He threatened to kill you if I didn't go." I can see he's going to ask another question, so I add, "He sent me photos of you. I thought if I could just get to CRC and have him focus on me, the guards there would be able to stop him."

"Jamie," he whispers as he turns onto his side so he can face me, "you're so unbelievably brave."

I didn't expect him to say that.

"I'm glad you think so," I try to joke. "Most people would call me stupid."

"Why do you think that?" He lifts a hand to my face, and brushes a finger from my cheek, down to my jaw.

"I just... Hell, even Henry said I was stupid to go to him."

He shakes his head lightly. "You came face to face with a monster, and you survived. You're such an incredible person." He presses a light kiss to my lips then smiles, "I should've known you were remarkable the night we argued, and you didn't back down."

Remembering the night I begin to smile, but then I freeze as a memory flashes through me.

"Oh, my God," I gasp as I sit up.

Julian shoots up as well. "What?"

"The night we argued, and I ran after you to apologize." I cover my mouth with my hand for a moment as I try to process it.

Julian shakes his head. "We dealt with all of that, didn't we?" he asks, misunderstanding my reaction.

"No, I don't mean about the argument itself. That night I ran into Henry's cart. I smiled and apologized to him before going after you, but..." I try to think if that could be it. "Do you think that's the moment that started this whole nightmare?"

Julian thinks back, then begins to nod. "It could be. It was your first night at Trinity."

"Right?"

I don't know why, but the realization makes me feel emotional. As if finding out where it all started helped to make the whole nightmare come full circle.

Julian pulls me closer and wraps his arms around me, then says, "It's over now. He will never hurt you again."

I nod as I move my arms around his neck, and taking in a deep breath of him, I close my eyes and whisper, "Thank you so much for standing by me through it all."

When I pull back, I see a smile tug at his mouth. "Jamie..." he tilts his head, his eyes filled with warmth as he looks at me, "will you go on a date with me?"

A grin spreads over my face. "I'd love to."

Chapter 35

Julian

Preston has been keeping an eye on the web for any chatter about Henry Little, but luckily, there hasn't been any.

The first three days were stressful, wondering if we might've missed anything, but Hayden assured me he and Max took care of the evidence.

Before they headed home to Virginia, I made a substantial donation to their foundation as a show of gratitude.

I'm busy putting on my tie for my date with Jamie when my phone rings.

"Julian Reyes," I answer.

The liaison at reception, says, "Sir, there's a Detective Olsen asking to see you."

Fuck.

Knowing I can't avoid him, I answer, "Send him up."

I finish perfecting my tie, then shrug on my jacket.

Jamie comes out of the bathroom, putting on an earring.

"Detective Olsen is here," I say. She freezes, and I see a flash of fear on her face. Closing the distance between us, I lift my hands and frame her face. "Don't worry about a thing. All you have to say is that you haven't heard from Little again."

"Okay."

Taking a step back, I glance down at the pale blue cocktail dress she's wearing. "You look absolutely breathtaking."

My compliment brings a smile to her face. "Thank you."

Taking hold of her hand, I say, "Let's handle this so we can go on our date."

Just as we walk into the living room, there's a knock. I take Jamie over to the sofa. "Sit down while I get the door."

Opening the door for him, I move back so he can enter. "Detective, please come in."

"Evening, folks. Sorry for coming over so late and not calling beforehand," he says as he glances around. "We've linked Henry Little to twelve homicides that were previously ruled suicide. I felt you should know."

Jamie told me he confessed to seventeen. I swallow the bitterness of the news down and say, "Thank you for letting us know."

"Unfortunately, we haven't been able to find any leads on his whereabouts. It's possible he fled the state."

Detective Olsen locks eyes with me for a moment too long, and it makes unease dart down my spine.

"We'll be careful." I keep my reply short, not wanting to arouse any suspicion.

The Detective glances around again, then asks, "Where are your guards?"

"They left. It was only a temporary arrangement." I see the question forming on his face, and add, "We still have our usual security."

"Oh, good." He glances at Jamie and asks, "How are you holding up, Miss Truman?"

Jamie smiles at the man, and her voice is steady when she answers, "I'm much better. Thank you for asking."

The detective nods, then looks at me again. "I'll keep you updated should we learn anything new."

"We'd appreciate that." I walk him to the door and reach out my hand to him.

As we shake, he stares at me again for a long moment. "I don't reckon we'll find him, huh? That's alright by me. Less paperwork."

His words catch me off guard, but I recover quickly and reply, "One can only hope."

He smiles one last time. "You keep well."

"You, too."

I watch as he walks away, sure that he knows I killed Little.

Was that his way of telling me, I don't need to worry?

"That went better than I thought it would," Jamie whispers from behind me.

I turn to her and seeing her relieved smile, I say, "Yes, it did. How about that date?"

She walks toward me and asks, "Where are we going?"

I wrap my arm around her waist and press a kiss to her lips. "You're going down to the restaurant. I have a table reserved for us."

"Me? Why? Where are you going?"

The corner of my mouth lifts, "I'll be down shortly."

"Okay." She gives me a confused look, then walks out and says, "Weirdest start to a date I've ever had."

Jamie

When the host seats me at the same table I sat at when I met Julian, I let out a chuckle. It looks like Julian reserved the entire restaurant because all the other tables are empty.

"Would you like to order something to drink?" A waiter asks.

"A virgin strawberry daiquiri, please." It's the same drink I had back then.

My eyes stay on the door, and when Julian walks in, a wide smile stretches across my face. He walks to the piano and sits down before he glances my way.

For a moment, he stares at me, then he glances down at the keys and begins to play.

It's the melody I love so much, and when the intro is done, he looks over to me with tenderness.

My heart melts for this man.

Maybe my judge of character is not off. The moment I saw Julian, I knew he was different from any other man.

His strength.

Oh, God, his loyalty.

Tears well in my eyes as emotion fills my chest.

I love him. Not because he killed for me. I love him because he never left my side.

By the time he stops playing, it's safe to say I've just fallen for him all over again.

My eyes follow Julian as he crosses the floor to the table. When he reaches me, he leans down and presses a soft kiss to my mouth before he takes a seat next to me.

"I thought we could give our first night together another try," he says.

A waiter comes to take our orders, and once he leaves, Julian reaches for my hand and wraps his fingers over mine.

"Tell me about yourself."

Not knowing where to start, I ask, "What would you like to know?"

"Anything. Where you went to school. About your life in Saluda."

I relax back in the chair. "Saluda." A nostalgic smile settles on my face. "It's a small town, but I loved it there. People greeted each other in passing. It's something that's lost in the bigger cities."

Moving our joined hands to his thigh, Julian turns his body toward me, and leaning his elbow on the table, he rests his chin on his thumb.

Having his complete attention, I continue, "I didn't know my dad, but everyone in town spoke of him with fondness. My mom…" I try to remember her and frown. "She worked a lot, and after her passing, we lived with Sue, who owned the diner my mother worked at." My smile widens even though there's a pang of sadness in my chest. "Sue never took anyone's crap." I let out a chuckle, but then my smile fades. "I miss her the most." I let out a breath then ask, "What about you?"

There's a soft smile playing around Julian's mouth that never fades even though he seems to be deep in thought.

"My life," he pauses, then shakes his head, "You know my mother has been charged with the attempted murder of Layla. The trial should come to a close in the next couple of weeks."

I give his hand a squeeze. "That must be very difficult for you to deal with."

He nods. "The media frenzy is the worst." He tilts his head. "Come to think of it, that's maybe why we managed to keep our relationship under wraps. The media is too focused on Clare's trial to notice anything else… for now."

"At least something good came from it. If the media had gotten wind of Little…" I shake my head as I take a deep breath, "That would've been catastrophic."

"They're bound to find out about our relationship soon," Julian warns. "Especially if they see me with a woman. Are you ready for that?"

I think about his question, then say, "I don't follow the news, but surely you've been seen with other women?"

Julian slowly shakes his head. "I've been too focused on CRC."

Frowning, I stare at him. "So, you haven't dated?"

He shakes his head again. "Not since Jennifer passed away."

"You were engaged to her, right?" I ask, hoping he'll talk about her. She had to be an amazing woman for Julian to want to marry her.

"Yes, she passed a couple of weeks before our wedding." He shifts in the chair, and his smile fades a little. "I'll always treasure the memories I have of her."

I hold his hand tighter.

He lets out a deep breath, then asks again, "Getting back to the topic of the media. I'm a very private person, but they're bound to find out. Are you ready for that?"

I hate being in the spotlight.

My eyes drift over Julian's face. Having gotten to know him over the last couple of weeks, I learned he's as strong as he looks. His brown eyes change shades depending on his mood. Darker for angry and looking like melted chocolate when he's relaxed. His arms have become my shelter against the world.

Realizing just how much I love him, I say, "I'll face all the press in the world for you."

My words make his face light up as his smile stretches wide.

Chapter 36

Julian

While enjoying our dinner, we begin to talk about random things again, and it lightens the weight of the past month.

"Do you love the mountains or the ocean more?" I ask.

Jamie let's out a chuckle. "Before all this happened, I would've said the mountains, but now it's definitely the ocean, frizzy hair and all."

She draws a burst of laughter from me.

"And you?"

Setting my utensils down, I move the plate to the side and first take a sip of whiskey before I answer, "Wherever you are."

She blinks at me a couple of times, then teases, "Wow, I forgot what a charmer you can be."

When she pushes her own plate aside, I wait for the waiter to clear the table, then I reach for her hand again. I bring it to my knee and glancing down, I lightly trace over her fingers with my other hand.

A John Legend song begins to play, and the corner of my mouth lifts, as I bring my eyes to Jamie's, "Would you like to go up to the suite and have conversations in the dark?"

She lets out a burst of laughter, and it has me staring at how beautiful she looks right now.

"I thought you'd never ask."

Standing up, I wait for Jamie to rise as well before I place my hand on her lower back. As we leave the restaurant and cross the floor of the lobby, I begin to feel the anticipation of spending the night with Jamie.

Waiting for the elevator to come down, she mumbles, "It moves so slow."

When the doors finally open, I wait for Jamie to step inside first. Following behind her, I swipe my card and press the number for the top floor.

Jamie leans back against the panel, and the sight makes my heart beat faster. I close the distance between us, and taking hold of her hip, I pull her to me. I bring my other hand to her neck and lightly brush over her skin. All the marks have faded from around her throat, but I'll never forget what they looked like.

My eyes find hers, and the moment is so very different from our first night together. Back then, there was only desire. But as I stare into the blue eyes of the woman that's become my life, everything feels much more intense.

I no longer only want her. I now need her, because without her my life and everything in it will be worthless.

The doors open, and as we step out, I pull her close to my side, our hands intertwined.

Once we walk into the suite, I shut the door behind us. When I turn my attention back to Jamie, there's a poignant expression on her face, making her look vulnerable.

"What are you thinking?" I ask, needing to know where her mind's at.

She lets out a trembling breath, before admitting, "I just realizing what I almost lost." She takes a step closer to me. "Not being able to smell your scent." Lifting a hand, she places it against my jaw. "Not seeing you again… touching you." Standing on her tiptoes, she presses a kiss to my mouth, then murmurs, "I'm so unbelievably grateful that I get to have this moment with you."

Raising my hands, I frame her face and stare deep into her eyes. "I'll treasure every day I get to have with you."

I lower my head and pressing my mouth to hers, I thank the powers that be that my prayers were answered.

Pulling back, I take her hand and lead her to the bedroom.

Removing my jacket, I throw it over the armchair, then I lift a hand to the back of Jamie's neck. "I want to wake up next to you."

Smiling at me, she teases, "I've been waking up next to you for almost two weeks."

I shake my head lightly. "I'm not talking about the past. I mean tomorrow and the day after, and every day after that."

"But I have to go back to school," she whispers. There's a puzzled look on her face.

"Am I moving too fast for you?" I ask, not wanting to pressure her into anything she's not ready for.

"No." She takes a deep breath and glances down before asking, "Are you asking me to stay here?"

I nudge her face back up so she'll look at me. "Yes."

"You want us to live together?" she asks again.

I let out a chuckle. "Yes."

"Oh, wow, I didn't expect that," she admits. "I thought I'd be returning to Trinity after this weekend."

"Do you want to go back to the dorm?" I ask, trying to brace myself for if she answers yes. I lower my hands from her face as I wait for her to respond.

"No," she whispers. A playful smile forms around her mouth. "I should warn you, though, I'm messy."

"We can have them clean the suite daily," I murmur as I begin to lower my head to hers.

"I don't have a car to get to classes."

Lightly, I brush my lips over hers. "No need for one. I'll arrange a driver for you and your guards."

"Guards?" she murmurs against my mouth, her eyelashes lowering with desire.

"I'm never leaving you unprotected again."

She pushes up against me, and her mouth presses harder against mine.

I wrap an arm around her, pulling her body right against mine as my tongue slips into her mouth.

I promise to keep you safe.

The kiss is fast and hungry but then eases to slow and intense, as our breaths mingle.

You are the reason my heart keeps beating.

I intensify the kiss, moving a hand to the back of her head where the gash has healed, but I keep my touch gentle.

Jamie's the one to break the kiss as she pulls back. She lifts her hand to my chest and begins to unbutton my shirt.

"I've wanted to do this for a while now," she admits, her voice soft and filled with desire.

The corner of my mouth lifts when she takes her time, brushing her hands over my bare arms as she pushes the shirt off.

When her hands drop to my belt, I reach for her and unzipping the back of her dress, I push the fabric from her shoulders, letting it fall to her feet.

Once our clothes are scattered over the floor, I whisper, "The only thing I want is to be with you, as close as I can be."

Jamie steps forward and pressing her body against mine, she wraps her hand around the back of my neck and slowly pulls me down to her as our eyes never leave each other.

Our mouths touch, and then there's only us. My heartbeat speeds up, and I wrap my arms around her. My fingers brush lightly up her back, and it makes her shiver against me. Slipping a hand into her hair, I tighten my hold on her as I deepen the kiss. Our tongues explore each other, soft then hungrily, and it pushes me to the edge of losing control, but I want this night to be special.

I pull her toward the bed, and for a moment, our mouths separate as she sits down, scooting back over the covers.

Breathless, I stare down at her. Seeing the same need on her face has me placing a knee on the mattress.

She opens her legs as I move in between them and I first place a kiss to the inside of her thigh, before I brush my lips over her skin until I reach the sensitive area above her opening. I begin to nip and suck at her and being overwhelmed by my hunger for her, I don't stop until my lips are tingling and she's writhing beneath me. Pressing a finger against her opening, I rub hard circles around it until her body tenses, and she lets out a moan as she orgasms.

Leaving her for a moment, I reach over to the bedside table and pull a box of condoms from the top drawer. Grabbing one, I tear the foil open using my teeth, then quickly roll it on.

Crawling over Jamie, I keep myself braced on my left arm, and I place my right on her hip. She stares up at me, her expression intense as she brings her hands to my shoulders.

Everything I feel reflects on her face. Leaning down, I close my mouth over hers and kiss her with every ounce of love I'm feeling.

I don't want to live without her. I can't breathe without her next to me.

I move my hand up over her ribs and cupping her breast, I knead her flesh until our bodies writhe against each other, needing more. I slide my hand back down and taking hold of myself, I rub over her slickness before I align myself with her opening.

My gaze drifts over her face before settling on her eyes. For a moment, we only stare at each other, then I whisper, "You're everything I've ever wanted but didn't know I needed."

Her eyes begin to shimmer in the dim light. I press a soft kiss to her mouth, and murmur, "I love you, Jamie."

Chapter 37

Jamie

My body begins to tremble from feeling overwhelmed by the significant moment we're sharing.

A lump pushes up my throat, making it impossible to say the words back to him. Instead, I lift my hand to the back of his neck and pull him down to me until our foreheads touch.

There's a heartbreaking look on Julian's face as he pushes inside me, and it makes tears escape my eyes.

When he's fully inside me, I manage to whisper with a quivering voice, "I love you so much."

Julian presses his mouth to mine, his eyes drifting closed as if he's soaking up the words I just said. His hips pull back, and when he pushes into me again, his eyes open, burning into me with intensity.

This is the moment we fought so hard for. This is what I feared losing the most.

Getting to be with Julian and having a future with him.

Julian begins to kiss my tears away as our bodies start to move together. I'm swept up in my emotions of making love to Julian, and when he moves faster, it steals my ability to breathe.

I wrap my arms around his neck, clinging to him – my lifeline and the only place I feel safe.

The rampant emotions begin to calm down a little, and I feel his toned body move against mine. Every time he thrusts inside me, it makes the pleasure begin to grow in my abdomen.

Our eyes never leave each other as we find our release together.

Julian's movements steadily slow down until he stills against me. His gaze caresses my face, and then he whispers, "I'll be right back."

I climb under the covers as Julian uses the restroom, then he switches off the light before coming to bed.

I wait for him to lie down before I snuggle closer. Once he wraps his arms around me, I let out a contented sigh.

He presses a kiss to my hair, then positions us, so we're lying face to face. He leans in and presses another kiss to my mouth, then whispers, "You're so beautiful."

When he kisses me again, I begin to smile.

"And brave."

Kiss.

"And intelligent."

Kiss.

"And everything I ever wanted in the woman I want to spend my life with."

My smile fades as tears begin to well in my eyes. "You're going to make me cry," I try to playfully chastise him, but when he looks at me with so much tenderness and love, I can't control the overpowering feelings bursting in my heart.

He pulls me to him, and I bury my face in his neck as my shoulders begin to shudder. I let the tears wash all the fear and trauma away, and in its place, hope for a beautiful future with Julian begins to grow.

Waking up, I feel Julian's warm skin beneath my cheek and snuggling closer, a contented smile pulls at my lips.

He tightens his arms around me, and his voice is rough from sleep as he murmurs, "This is the best feeling in the world."

I press a kiss to his chest. "Can we stay in bed all day?"

"Hmm… tempting, but we have dinner with the group tonight."

"Oh yeah, it's Sunday," I mumble, then let out a happy sigh.

"I think we should swing by Trinity and get the rest of your stuff so you can return to classes tomorrow without having to worry about it."

I shift my head and glance up at Julian. "Yeah, I suppose I have to get that done sooner or later. Then Preston can move back into his room."

"You want to shower first while I order us some coffee?"

I push up into a sitting position, and the covers slip back, exposing my body.

Julian's eyes drop to my breasts, and reaching up, he brushes his knuckle over my nipple.

"Or we can stay in bed the whole day," I tease.

He sits up and presses a hard kiss to my mouth, then climbs out of bed. "No, I have other plans for you."

When I open the door to the suite I shared with Layla and
Kingsley, and I step inside, Kingsley's head snaps up from
where she was concentrating on her laptop screen.

The moment she sees me, she drops her lollipop on the
table and jumping up, she shrieks, "Oh my God, you're
here!" She runs over to me and grabbing me into a hug, she
shouts, "Layla, Jamie's back!"

She holds me at arm's length and lets her eyes scan
over me. "Are you okay? We wanted to come visit, but
Julian asked us to give you some time." She shoots him a
scowl before a wide smile splits over her face again.

Layla comes out of her room and takes hold of
Kingsley's arm, pulling her back. "Let them at least come
inside."

I shut the door behind us.

"I'll be in your room," Julian says and presses a kiss to
my temple before he walks away.

Kingsley instantly grins at me.

Layla glances after Julian before she looks at me. "How
are you? Have the police said anything?"

Oh crap, they don't know Henry's dead.

"They think Henry skipped town," I say so they won't
worry about me.

"Yuck… just hearing his name." Kingsley gets the shivers while pulling a disgusted face.

"But you're okay now?" Layla asks again.

"Yeah, I'm much better. Julian's been amazing and is taking care of me."

"So…" Kingsley wiggles her eyebrows, "are you a couple now?"

"Of course, they are," Layla says. "She's been living at his place for a while now."

"Are you coming back to school?" Kingsley asks.

I nod. "I'll return to classes tomorrow. We actually came to get the rest of my belongings so Preston can have his room back."

Kingsley's mouth drops open, and Layla's eyes widen.

Layla seems to recover first. "You're moving in with him?"

When I nod, Kingsley lets out an excited shriek, and then she hugs me again. "I'm so happy for you."

Suddenly Julian says from where he's standing in my bedroom's doorway, "Falcon doesn't know. I'd appreciate it if you let me tell him."

"Of course," Layla answers. She glances from Julian to me, then says, "You have no idea how happy I am to know you're together."

Walking over to Julian, she gives him a hug and whispers something to him before she lets him go.

"We'll still have our dinners on Sundays, right?" Kingsley asks.

"Yes, definitely," I reply, appreciating how supportive the girls are. "I'm going to pack quickly."

When I walk past Julian, I take hold of his hand and pull him into the room with me.

When we're alone, I ask, "What did Layla say to you?"

Julian walks to my dresser and opening it, he begins to remove the remainder of my clothes.

"She just said she's happy for me and that I deserve a chance at happiness."

I smile widely at the words. "She's right."

I begin folding the clothes and placing them in the bag Julian just put down on the bed.

He pauses and watching me closely, he asks, "When we're done loading everything in the car, would you like to go for a piano lesson?"

I glance down at the shirt in my hands and swallow before I answer, "Sure, sounds like a good idea."

Julian takes his phone from his pocket, and I watch with a frown as he dials a number.

"Afternoon, it's Julian. Can you clear the music center at two for me?" My eyebrows pop up. "Thank you."

When he tucks the phone back in his pocket, I say, "You didn't have to do that. We only need the one studio."

Julian just smiles at me. "We only have thirty minutes. Let's get this done."

Chapter 38

Julian

When we have Jamie's belongings loaded in my car, we walk down the path leading to the music building. I place my arm around her shoulders and draw her against my side, pressing a kiss to her hair.

Students stare as we pass them, and then a group of girls approaches us. "Jamie, we haven't seen you in a while," the one says as her eyes dart between us before resting a couple of seconds too long on me.

"Uh… yeah," Jamie answers, her voice tight, which tells me she's not friends with them.

"We should have lunch," the girl says.

I have to search my memory for her name and which family she belongs to.

Cynthia Healey? No, that's her mother's name.

Giving up on trying to remember the girl's name, I keep my tone professional, as I say, "Miss Healey, you'll have to excuse us."

I begin to walk, and when she doesn't move, my expression turns to a scowl. "Move."

"Oh, sure." She finally moves out of the way.

I feel irritated, and when we reach the building, I ask, "Do you know them?"

"No, I only spoke to them once," Jamie says, sounding annoyed. "I'm really going to throat punch her. There's just something about her that aggravates the living hell out of me."

Unable to stop, I chuckle at her response. When she glances up at me, I say, "Trust me to fall madly in love with a spit-fire."

"Yeah?" she grins, the other girls now forgotten.

Walking into the studio, I shut the door behind us and lock the door, so we won't be disturbed.

"Are you going to teach me something new today?" Jamie asks as she walks to the piano.

"Hold up." She pauses and turns back to me as I move toward her. Standing in front of her, I say, "I need you naked for what I want to show you."

She begins to laugh, then takes a step back. The smile on her face is absolutely stunning as she wiggles out of her underwear and sweatpants. Her expression changes as desire settles on her face.

When she pulls her shirt over her head, I close the distance between us and bring a hand to her jaw. My mouth crashes down on hers, and the kiss quickly turns heated and breathless.

Breaking the kiss for a moment, I push her back until we reach the bench. "Sit on the piano with your feet on the bench."

"I really like this lesson," she teases as she sits down.

I place my hand on her thigh as I climb over the bench. Taking a seat between her legs, I look up at her, drinking in how breathtaking she looks with her lips parted before I lower my eyes to her abdomen.

Leaning forward, I press a kiss to the inside of her thigh before I move to her opening, and I begin teasing her with my tongue.

She gasps when I nip at her bundle of nerves, and then I suck and nibble until her thighs are shaking under my hands, and she explodes over my tongue.

Sitting back, I remove a condom from my pocket and unzip my jeans. In a hurry to be inside her, I push the fabric down and freeing my cock, I roll on the condom.

I rise to my feet and wrap an arm around Jamie's waist, lifting her to my body. I move us to the side of the piano and set her down on top of the dark wood.

Her breaths are still rushing from her parted lips as I position my cock at her entrance, then I growl, "Hold on to me."

She shifts as close to me as she can, wrapping her arms around my neck, and then I thrust forward and sinking into her warmth, my breaths falter.

Being inside Jamie, there's no feeling in the world that can rival it.

Locking eyes with her, I keep the pace hard and fast. The sounds of our pelvises meeting fill the room, along with moans of pleasure, and it sounds like music to my ears.

"Julian," she gasps, and releasing my neck, she places her hands behind her on the piano, which gives me a perfect view of her breasts. My eyes drift down her body, and I watch as I drive back inside her. The sight is unbelievable, and it pushes me over the edge.

My hips keep moving as I find my release, and needing Jamie to orgasm again, I slip a hand between us and begin to rub hard on her bundle of nerves.

Her hands buckle from under her, and she falls back on the wood, arching her back as her body tightens with release.

My movements slow as I stare at Jamie while she comes down from her orgasm.

"Do you have any idea how fucking breathtaking you look right now."

She tries to chuckle while catching her breath.

"I could make love to you all day long," she says as she pushes herself back up into a sitting position.

"That's the plan for after dinner." Lifting my hand to the back of her neck, I pull her face to mine and press a tender kiss to her lips. "Time for that piano lesson now."

Jamie

After leaving Trinity, we stopped at the store so I could get some feminine products.

I've just finished unpacking everything, and while Julian returns a business call he missed, I decide to phone Della and Carter.

"Hey, I was just about to call you," Della answers. "How are you?"

"I'm doing much better. How are you, and Carter, and the kids?" I ask quickly before Della asks more questions.

"We're well. Danny's excited for her new little brother to make his appearance, and I have to admit I'm way past the point of ready for him to come now."

I hate that I'm not going to be there for Tristan's birth.

"I wish I could be there," I express my thoughts.

"Me too," Della murmurs. "Have the police said anything new about the case?"

Do I tell Della?

I decide not to, wanting to spare her the distress of something that's in the past now.

"They think Henry left the state," I say so she'll stop worrying about him.

"Really?" She lets out a breath, then asks, "How do they know, though?"

"Detective Olsen didn't go into specifics, but he seemed pretty sure I'm no longer in danger. Julian still has personal guards for me, so you don't need to worry."

"That's a relief, then." Pausing for a moment, I hear her yell at Danny to stop jumping on the couch, then she asks, "How's school? Have you managed to catch up on all your work?"

"It's going well. Lake is helping me with my assignments."

"That's nice of him."

Knowing I'll have to tell her at some point, I decide to just go for it. "I'm not staying at the dorms any longer."

"Why? Where are you staying now?" I can hear the apprehension in her voice.

"I moved in with Julian."

"Oh…" she lets out a sigh. "You had me worried there for a moment. I thought you moved into an apartment on your own."

Frowning, I ask, "So you don't mind that I'm living with Julian?"

"No, why would I?"

"Oh, I just assumed you'd be upset or think it's too soon."

"Jamie, you're levelheaded, and I trust you to make the right decisions. If you care that much about Julian, then go for it. Your happiness is all that matters to me."

I sit down on the armchair, feeling relieved that Della is okay with it all. "How do you think Carter's going to react?"

"Ask him yourself. He's standing right here."

"What? No! Wait!"

I freeze as I hear Della handing the phone to Carter.

"Hey, Jamie," his voice comes over the line, and it has me grinning sheepishly even though he can't see my face.

"Hey, Carter. How are you?"

"Good. I wanted to ask whether I should send the private jet for you on Friday. Della's scheduled to be induced then, and I thought you'd want to be here."

I didn't even think of that. "That would be awesome."

"Great, I'll let you know the time." He pauses for a moment then asks, "So what's this about you and Julian?"

Slumping back in the chair, I cover my eyes with my other hand. "We moved in together."

"You did? Hmm…"

Sitting up straight, I ask, "What does hmm mean?"

"Just me thinking."

I scowl at his answer. "Don't you approve of my relationship with him?"

Just as I ask the question, Julian comes to stand in the doorway and leans against the jamb.

"I didn't say that. Even though I wanted to punch him a couple of times, it's clear he cares about you. I'm just worried that you're moving too fast with everything that's happened."

My eyes meet Julian's as I say, "I'm sure of my feelings, Carter."

"Then there's nothing more to say on the matter. Like Della said, the only thing that counts is your happiness."

"Thanks, Carter." I let out a sigh and relax again.

"Tell Julian to take good care of you." I hear the warning in Carter's voice.

"He does take good care of me. You don't need to worry about that."

"Good. I need to go, but we'll see you on Friday, right?"

"Yes, I'll see you Friday. Have a great week, and give Danny and Christopher a kiss from me."

"Will do."

When I cut the call, Julian saunters closer. "What did they say about us living together?"

I shrug as I stand up. "They're okay with it."

"Really?" Julian's eyebrow rises.

"Yes, really," I chuckle. "I'm going to get ready for dinner." Pressing a kiss to his lips, I walk over to the ensuite bathroom to shower.

Chapter 39

Julian

I've asked Falcon to come up to the suite before dinner, and as I open the door for him, I smile.

"Come in." Not seeing Layla, I ask, "Are you alone?"

"Yeah, Layla's downstairs with Kingsley. She thought we might want to have some privacy."

"Great, let's go to my study."

"Where's Jamie?" Falcon asks as he follows me.

"She's still getting ready." When we walk into the study, I gesture to a chair. "Take a seat."

Once we're comfortable, I lean forward and rest my elbows on my thighs.

"Why did you want to see me in private?" Falcon asks, his eyes scanning over my face.

"I wanted to tell you that Jamie has moved in permanently."

Falcon only chuckles to the news. "I figured that would happen." Smiling at me, he asks, "Are there any new developments with the case."

I take a deep breath. "That's the other thing I wanted to talk about." My eyes rest on Falcon.

Falcon, Mason, and Lake need to know the truth. They'd never leave it alone otherwise.

"Something happened during the week." I'm not sure how to go about telling him, so I just say, "I shot and killed Henry Little."

I watch as the shock vibrates over my little brother's face, and for an instant, it makes me regret having told him.

"What happened?" he asks once he's processed what I just told him.

"He lured Jamie away with the threat of killing me if she didn't go to him. We found them in time, and I shot him. There's no way I could let him live."

The worry on his face is palpable as he asks, "Is Jamie okay?"

"She's fine. She was shaken up, but she's dealing as well as can be expected with the trauma."

Falcon leans closer to me and places a hand on my shoulder. "And you? How are you dealing with everything that's happened?"

I close my eyes as the emotions from the nightmare roll over me again. "I'll be okay. It's just hard not to become too overprotective of Jamie. Whenever I'm not with her, I start to panic."

Falcon pulls me into a hug. "I'm here whenever you need to talk. I don't care what the time is."

Pulling back, I smile gratefully at him. "Thanks." I rise to my feet and say, "We should go. Lake has probably already ordered half the menu."

Falcon chuckles as we walk to the door, but then I stop him with a hand on his shoulder. "You can tell Mason and Lake things have been taken care of."

Knowing I can trust the three with my life, I know I won't have to worry about them telling anyone else.

When we walk into the living room, Jamie stands up from the couch. "Hey, Falcon."

My brother walks right over to her and engulfs her in a hug.

The sight of them holding each other is overwhelming. It makes me realize what I have to be thankful for.

An amazing girlfriend.

A brother who I can share my darkest secrets with and know he won't turn his back on me.

My breaths begin to speed up as emotion after emotion wash over me. It's impossible to describe the happiness I feel while I stare at everything I ever wanted.

Epilogue

Jamie

Three months later...

Reaching up, I adjust Julian's tie.

"Are you ready?" he asks, looking all calm and collected where it feels like a hundred bees are buzzing in my stomach.

"As ready as I'll ever be."

He smiles lovingly at me, then presses a kiss to my mouth. "Let's get this over with."

Julian takes hold of my hand and weaves our fingers together. I suck in a deep breath as we begin to walk toward the conference room in the hotel where the media are waiting.

The moment we walk through the door, cameras begin to flash, and I fight the urge to turn my face away from them.

Julian pulls out a chair and waits for me to sit before taking a seat next to me.

"Mr. Reyes and Miss Truman will only answer questions for ten minutes. After that, we ask that you respect their privacy," Stephanie announces. She gestures to a reporter in the front row. "Mr. Brown, the first question."

The media have been harassing us for this interview since they learned Julian and I were a couple.

"Congrats on your engagement," Mr. Brown begins. "Can I ask what impact the sentencing of Clare Reyes has had on your relationship?"

Julian clears his throat and leans closer to the microphone. "The trial had nothing to do with my relationship with Miss Truman. Next question."

I place my hand on Julian's thigh and give it a squeeze.

"How do you feel about your mother being sentenced to fifteen years for attempted murder?" Another reporter asks.

Julian's facial expression remains neutral as he answers, "The sentence was well deserved."

Luckily another reporter asks, "Miss Truman, how does it feel to be engaged to such a powerful man and one of California's most eligible bachelors?"

I take a deep breath before I answer, "I don't see Julian in that light. To me, he's the man I love."

A man in the front row asks, "Are you telling us the status that comes along with marrying Mr. Reyes means nothing to you?"

Seriously?

I smile, sweetly at the man. "Sir, at the end of the day, status means nothing. I love Julian because he's caring, loyal, and... he's everything to me."

"If a movie had to be made about your romance, who would you want the actors to be?"

I blink at the question, then begin to chuckle but quickly try and cover it up with a cough.

The questions keep coming until Stephanie steps forward. "That will be all. Thank you for joining us today."

As we rise from the chairs, reporters keep yelling questions. Holding his hand, I stick close to Julian's side as we walk toward our personal guards, who escort us out of the hotel to our waiting car.

Julian opens the door for me, and I slip into the back seat before he follows.

With all the media coverage our relationship has been getting, it has made it harder to move around, and Julian has insisted I have security with me at all times.

Joseph climbs behind the steering wheel while Brian gets in on the passenger side. As we pull away from the hotel to go home, I think back to how Julian proposed to me.

I didn't see it coming.

Because of our shared love for music, he flew us to New York, where we had a private performance by Hans Zimmer.

The night was out of this world, to say the least.

Julian dropped to his knee in old fashion style on the Bow Bridge in Central Park and promised his undying love to me.

I squealed.

Then I cried.

A smile forms around my lips, and it has Julian asking, "What are you thinking about?"

"Just how happy you make me." I place my hand on his knee.

Joseph pulls up the driveway of the Reyes mansion, and seeing Mr. Reyes sitting on the bench and reading a book, my smile widens.

A month ago, we moved into the mansion because Julian's father insisted a hotel was no place for us seeing as we were getting engaged. I was worried at first, but it was for nothing. Mr. Reyes has become the father I never had.

Climbing out of the car, I hook my arm through Julian's as we walk toward the front door.

This house is where we'll get married in two months' time.

This house is where we'll raise our children.

Stopping on the porch, I reach up and lightly frame Julian's jaw, and standing on my tiptoes, I press a kiss to his mouth. "I love you, Julian."

The End

Thank you for taking this incredible journey with me.

Trinity Academy

FALCON
Novel #1
Falcon Reyes & Layla Shepard

MASON
Novel #2
Mason Chargill & Kingsley Hunt

LAKE
Novel #3
Lake Cutler & Lee-ann Park

JULIAN
Novel #4
A Stand Alone Novel
Julian Reyes (*Falcon's Brother*)
&
Jamie Truman (*Della's Sister – Heartless, TETLS*)

THE EPILOGUE
Novel #5
The Epilogue will conclude the Trinity Academy series.

Enemies To Lovers

<u>Heartless</u>
Novel #1
Carter Hayes & Della Truman

<u>Reckless</u>
Novel #2
Logan West & Mia Daniels

<u>Careless</u>
Novel #3
Jaxson West & Leigh Baxter

<u>Ruthless</u>
Novel #4
Marcus Reed & Willow Brooks

<u>Shameless</u>
Novel #5
Rhett Daniels & Evie Cole

<u>False Perceptions</u>
Novel #6
A Stand Alone Novel
Hayden Cole *(Evie's Dad)*

The Next Generation

COMING 2020

HUNTER
Novel #1
Hunter Chargill (*Mason and Kingsley's son*)
&
Jade Daniels (*Rhett & Evie's daughter*)

KAO
Novel #2
Kao Reed (*Marcus and Willow's son*)
&
Fallon Reyes (*Falcon & Layla's daughter*)

NOAH
Novel #3
Noah West (*Jaxson & Leigh's son*)
&
Carla Reyes (*Julian & Jamie's daughter*)

RYKER
Novel #4
Ryker West (*Logan & Mia's son*)
&
Danny Hayes (*Carter & Della's daughter*)

CHRISTOPHER
Novel #5
Christopher Hayes – (*Carter & Della's son*)
&
Dash West – (*Jaxson & Leigh's daughter*)

FOREST
Novel #6
Forest Hayes (*Carter & Della's son*)
&
Aria Chargill (*Mason & Kingsley's daughter*)

TRISTAN
Novel #7
Tristan Hayes – (*Carter & Della's son*)
&
Hana Cutler – (*Lake & Lee's daughter*)

JASE
Novel #8
Jase – (*Julian & Jamie's son*)
&
Mila – (*Logan & Mia's Daughter*)

Connect with me

Newsletter

FaceBook

Amazon

GoodReads

BookBub

Instagram

Twitter

Website

About the author

Michelle Heard is a Bestselling Romance Author who loves creating stories her readers can get lost in. She loves an alpha hero who is not afraid to fight for his woman.

Want to be up to date with what's happening in Michelle's world? Sign up to receive the latest news on her alpha hero releases → NEWSLETTER

If you enjoyed this book or any book, please consider leaving a review. It's appreciated by authors.

Acknowledgments

Sheldon, you're my everything.

To my beta readers, Kelly, Elaine, and Sarah – Thank you for being the godparents of my paper-baby.

Leeann, Sheena, and Allyson – Thank you for listening to me ramble, for reading and rereading the Trinity Academy series with me.

Sherrie, my sister from another mister. Girl, without you, I'd be a mess. Thank you for being the first person I speak to every morning, and the last before I go to sleep. I hope I get to hug you one day.

Candi Kane PR - Thank you for being patient with me and my bad habit of missing deadlines.

Wander & Andrew – Thank you for giving Julian the perfect look.

A special thank you to every blogger and reader who took the time to take part in the cover reveal and release day.

Love ya all tons ;)

Printed in Great Britain
by Amazon

21692140R00190